LOSING CAMILLE

stories

Paul Kilgore

Black Lawrence Press
www.blacklawrence.com

Executive Editor: Diane Goettel
Book Design: Steven Seighman

Black Lawrence Press
115 Center Avenue
Pittsburgh, PA 15215
U.S.A.

"Welcome to My World" appeared in Prairie Schooner.

"Elders" and "Roeschler's Home" appeared in Minnesota Monthly; "Roeschler's Home" was the winner of the Tamarack Award for Short Fiction.

Excerpt from "The First Dream" from The Art of Drowning, by Billy Collins, © 1995. Reprinted by permission of the University of Pittsburgh Press.

Published 2010 by Black Lawrence Press, an imprint of Dzanc Books

First edition March, 2010
ISBN-13: 978-0-9815899-8-5
Printed in the United States

Table of Contents

For Becky, Emily, and Mara
and for my parents,
all of them supportive and loving

The wind is ghosting around the house tonight,
as I lean against the door of sleep
I begin to think about the first person to dream,
how quiet he must have seemed the next morning ...

Billy Collins,
"The First Dream"

Elders

God found me – found all of us – the year of my twelfth birthday. We used a twenty-two to shoot Joseph and Josephine and abandoned a life that had not been a bad life. But Arthur Backstrom promised better.

This was 1971, the year of the Pentagon Papers and the convictions of Lieutenant Calley and Charles Manson both. Arthur Backstrom, like Jesus, was a carpenter. He signed a contract to acquire the long-empty Dahl Hotel and convinced forty men to rehabilitate it so that hundreds more of us could move in. Convincing was Arthur Backstrom's genius. He was only seven years to town but had built up a following by visiting the churches – all Protestant, this being the northern plains – and questioning the children. "What about this?" he would ask a group of high school boys as they punched their arms into letter jackets and stepped from the church into the iodine light of earliest spring. *This* was 1 Timothy 6:16, on display in the open Bible Backstrom held forth: "The Lord only hath immortality, dwelling in the light which no man can approach unto." "How," Arthur Backstrom asked, "can we read this and leave our faith" – with aversion he would nod back toward the church, rendering it feeble yet somehow oppressive – "as an hour-a-week proposition?"

It was through the students that Backstrom spoke to the parents. Most turned away, first in patronizing dismissal, later in fear. Arthur Backstrom often used a church's collection plates as his props. "Is this what we would give to our God?" he would ask, loudly, of a boy near him in the back pews. "Coffee money?" By then the plate he was holding aloft had made the rounds and indeed held little more than a litter of one- and five-dollar bills. I saw it happen in our church and similar stories filled the school hallways. The presiding minister invariably agreed with Backstrom's sentiments but was shaken by the disruption. A Lutheran pastor once asked him to leave; Backstrom left without protest. Arthur Backstrom made a point of demonstrating respect for authority.

Glen Opseth was one of the first to listen. He was a year into college and on a weekend home debated Backstrom eagerly over the meaning of baptism. We – a half-ring of boys surrounded by a half-ring of men – crowded into the narthex to watch. The mothers and wives were behind us; they and Arthur Backstrom, to the end, had reason to regard one another with suspicion. I suppose the men, hidden from our view, joined the boys in seeing the performance – valiant Opseth succumbing to a perfectly reasonable Arthur Backstrom – as theater. My father was among them. Within a week Opseth took a job at Backstrom's small farm.

My mother's friends were alarmed by Backstrom, though she – who I know now would have understood my father's vulnerability long before I sensed what was to befall us – said nothing when these women carried the town's raging allegations into our home. "What he calls discussion is what anyone else would call hypnosis," Marion Whitley said. By this time seven or eight families had moved onto the Backstrom farm. Hypnosis seemed plausible: half of those families had gone to rescue persuaded children but stayed, persuaded themselves. "The thing to do," I remember hearing Mrs. Whitley say, "is to not let him look you in the eye. His power is in his eyes. And never" – this was the most common and emphatic warning one heard – "let him begin a conversation with the young people." Convincing, everyone knew from even the earliest days, was Arthur Backstrom's genius.

At twelve I was several years too young to be worth convincing. Arthur Backstrom knew my father was a plumber and spoke to him directly. He did this by coming to our converted farmhouse – since my grandmother's death there were just the three of us, living quietly in the home where my father had been raised – on a Sunday afternoon. We were watching baseball and felt foolish to have Backstrom, Bible in lap, among us. My father turned off the television and I wandered off in a fit of resentment. While living in the Upper Room – Backstrom's name for the entirety of the Dahl – I often looked back at that resentment as evidence of the emptiness of my life before Christ. I spent the afternoon doing things I would never do again, though of course I couldn't have known that then. I hit pitches from Roxy Martin. Showed the younger boys at the park how to dribble a basketball they kept kicking into the grass. I checked a muskrat trap I knew Charlie Kamrath kept along the pond near the cemetery. After each diversion I returned home to find Backstrom's aged truck still in our driveway.

He stayed for supper. This was what pastors did, and I always assumed Arthur Backstrom was a pastor, or had been a pastor, or had some sort of seminary education, though to this day I don't know if any of these things were true. He certainly knew his Bible. At supper he spoke of the Acts of the Apostles and how heady those early days of the church must have been, Christ's followers surrendering everything – property, family, self – to His will. What had happened? How had man let such a moment in history slip away? Arthur Backstrom, whose rimless glasses, kitetail tie, and Stetson would have camouflaged him in a crowd a decade earlier, but who by 1971 was becoming slightly dated, even in the backwater of Syfer – Arthur Backstrom spoke confidently but soberly: he made the fantastic sound sensible. The memory of my parents at that meal remains sharp. My father grew excited in a way new to me. Everything said so calmly by Backstrom seemed a revelation, as indisputably true and primordial as winter stars. My mother spoke little. So many times since I've attempted, without success, to recall the frown of doubt, the muted caution. It was not detectable.

After disposing of the cats – the outrage of a gun felt right, even to me; it was a necessary preparation for the wholesale disposal that was to follow – we moved into the Upper Room. A hundred had preceded us and many more were to follow. What the Ackbees needed – Apostolic Children of Belief we were, and permitted to speak of ourselves in shorthand – we gave: our tools, vehicles, furniture, title to the farmhouse. What wasn't needed was cast to Syfer's saturated market. The proceeds found their way to the Upper Room.

As more Ackbees arrived it was decreed that families would pair up and share rooms. The Hillmans had three boys close to me in age and Arthur Backstrom saw an advantage in the combination. All eight of us crowded into what for eighty years had been Room 309. Think of it as camping, my father said, or making friends during a stranding blizzard. Though in truth little of our time was spent in 309. The Ackbees had a rigorous schedule: the men had a community to build and operate, the women had all the usual supporting chores women had been placed on Earth to perform. Part of what the women did was teach. All the children had been pulled out of public schools and even in the summer our Ackbee classes ran through the day, English and Bible in the morning, math and more Bible in the afternoon. The entire community met in the evening, out on the lawn in warm weather, for services that were measured in hours. New arrivals were introduced – during one stretch this happened almost nightly. The Biblical commands that governed us were recited. No pants for women (Deuteronomy 22:5). No tattoos, the men were admonished (Leviticus 19:28), though I had never seen a tattoo and no one in Syfer knew how to burn one. No involvement with banks (Deuteronomy 23:19); paying off mortgages and closing accounts were in themselves sufficient reasons for selling our farms and homes. Those with beards could not trim them (Leviticus 19:27). (We all learned our Bible well. Randy Hillman, before we warmed to one another, sought to establish our respective roles by quoting to me from the twenty-third chapter of Deuteronomy: "He that is wounded in the stones, or hath his privy member cut off, shall not enter the congregation of the Lord.") Arthur Backstrom followed with a long and intricate sermon, remarkably untheatrical, though often delivered in a low rage. The service was void of music.

The Upper Room was two blocks from our small downtown, but we had otherwise abandoned Syfer – Spirit Hollow, Glen Opseth called it. The loss of so many purchasers was not taken well. Ackbees inspired mystery and apprehension, but mostly hatred. Boys I had known at school launched rocks from the sidewalk, often in the presence of their parents. Suspicious utility problems plagued the Upper Room. Removed as we were from our prior lives, there was no way to verify what we believed to be true – that the ministers spent their Sunday mornings denouncing us, that the local paper had asked the state to close the Dahl and scatter us. A half dozen Ackbee men stood guard through the nights. We seemed to be living in the cube of each day, as I remember it, not wondering how all of this would conclude itself.

We only left the Upper Room during the late night. In summer darkness – for hours, with midnight the fulcrum – Ackbees roamed up and down the sidewalks, conversing gently under hissing streetlights orbited by balls of dark leaves. Even a twelve-year-old was allowed this diversion. Large beetles emerged, I remember. A train of empty boxcars announced itself well in advance and eventually rolled its way through town. There were two police cars in Syfer then, and they shadowed us devoutly. The curious unconverted often watched from their lawns; occasionally a car horn or sputtered obscenity was directed our way. "Hope for you in heaven," we replied, gently. Arthur Backstrom had taught us this. Ackbees never initiated conversations, though the adults responded cheerfully, even joyously, to prospects. But there was no reason, Backstrom warned, for communication with old acquaintances or the merely inquisitive. We had left all of that behind. I measured my life as an Ackbee against the accumulation of a dozen years and did not find our new course abnormal. Old ways fell easily; exchanging routines seemed as natural as moving from one season to another. The Dahl soon felt familiar: the boom and rattle of the pipes inside its walls, as though a great monster had been encased and was settling toward the inevitable acceptance of its enslavement; the old building's complex aroma of mildew, sun-baked lumber, paint and plaster, the cellar smells of greens and soil among mason jars; and, most acutely, the unceasing nighttime activity outside our heavy door, footsteps following footsteps, a constant hallway light, thick and yellow, projecting itself through the high transom. From my corner cot the severe angle shaped the transom as a trapezoid; when I woke in the early morning the hallway light had faded into the gloom of pre-dawn, and at least once I fell back to sleep dreaming of a mirror dropped into a lake, the reflected noonday sunlight dissolving as the mirror slowly tumbled and sank into the darkening water.

Walls had been knocked down on the Dahl's top floor and the large room that resulted served as our classroom. Arthur Backstrom appeared one August morning and asked for me. The seven of us who would have been in seventh grade were in our corner with Hannah Backstrom, studying Ezekiel. For Arthur Backstrom to be among children during the scuttling single-mindedness of the morning was a rare thing, and ominous. "Luke," he spoke, watching me carefully. He said nothing more before the others, but when we were alone in the attic's storage room he recounted, precisely and accurately, what I had done. Then he described the harm such actions could cause – had, indeed, already caused. It was a sermon, I suppose. Backstrom said my recklessness made the punishment to be administered the most important thing he could be doing that morning, even among a fellowship of upwards of three hundred. He quoted Scripture. A tail of leather embedded with twelve bolts hung on the wall. After I had undressed Arthur Backstrom used this tail on me. The deliberate engineering of that tail – the call and response between leather and bolts – produced a swell of terror that seemed to rend soul and body.

Others had preceded me. Robbie Schwartz had stolen another Ackbee's money – something like ten or twelve dollars, I recall – and been beaten. Terry Pierson had been beaten, too. His transgression had involved skipping a day of instruction for no good reason. Both of these offenses were serious, but hardly as threatening to the Apostolic Children as what I had done.

My mother found me when she returned to 309 after helping prepare the noon meal. I was in bed but awake. Upon seeing me she gasped, first at the scandal of my being in 309 during the heart of midmorning responsibilities, then, as she drew closer, at the alteration of my shoulders and exposed arm and especially my swollen eyes and torn ear. She examined me rapidly. A washcloth white and soft as a spring rabbit was gathered; with a basin of water she tended to the welts. My mother made no effort to suppress her sobs. Hers was, I now understand, a dangerous courage.

The Hillmans stayed clear of the room that day and evening. I was kept in a fever by the fire of Backstrom's tail, and only intermittently aware of what was occurring about me. My parents, together, were present every time I was able to notice. "Buddy," my father said each time he came near. It was unclear whether we knew the same things about what had happened. Shame encircled us like disease.

I slept through that evening's service – slept through it in my bed, that is, sheltered from the curious or condemning stares of an entire community. The absence was permitted, perhaps demanded. The boy I saw in the mirror the next morning was misshapen, pockets of olive and jaundice pushing to the surface to resemble jaggedly-defined regions of an unfamiliar map. I endured morning classes – the long climb up the steep stairway, the whispers and adhering glances of children and adults alike – but spent the afternoon back in 309. A fine rain, largely silent, began to fall. The evening meal's shifts ran their course and then everyone gathered in the Dahl's large converted lobby for the service.

I cannot say, knowing what followed, whether my father's words were inevitable. I was merely the most recent in the gathering procession of examples pioneered by Schwartz and Pierson. Yet there was a procession. And a bolt had found the side of my face; there was no precedent for that. These twin events, violation and consequence, were steps that had churned, from the muddy Jordan, mushrooming billows incapable of being tracked to one foot at the expense of the other. This is what swirled around all of us. But I was twelve years old and expected nothing. All that followed was unanticipated, and I observed it without curiosity.

"Lord," my father said, slowly rising. This occurred three-quarters through the service, during community prayers. A half-dozen men had already spoken, asking for continued financial sustenance, alternating rain and sun for the large garden out back, health for an ailing member. "Lord," said my father, among the bowed heads of everyone he now cared for, "help us know that You are God, and to You alone belongs wisdom." And then: "Help us to resist being led astray by false gods and leaders."

Until the final words he could have been speaking of me and my breach. But at that last phrase, spoken so deliberately as to foreclose any suspicion of inadvertence – at *and leaders*, Arthur Backstrom rose to the pulpit with an air of danger about him. His voice, which each night brought community prayers to a close, ran straight to my father. "From the Book of Hebrews our Scriptures instruct us to obey our leaders and submit to their authority. From Jeremiah: 'I will punish you according to the fruit of your doings, saith the Lord.' From Deuteronomy, Chapter twenty-one . . . ." Here Arthur Backstrom turned fiercely to his Bible; there could be no tolerance of inexactitude. "'If a man have a stubborn and rebellious son,'" he read, "'which will not obey the voice of his father, or the voice of his mother, then shall his father and mother lay hold of him, and bring him out unto the elders of his city, and unto the gate of his place; and they shall say unto the elders of his city, This our son is stubborn and rebellious, he will not obey our voice; and all the men of his city shall stone him with stones, that he die.'" Arthur Backstrom looked up from Deuteronomy, but not at my father. Instead he spoke to the church as one, quoting each word as its own sentence: "'So shalt thou put evil away from among you.'"

I remember few original words from Arthur Backstrom that night. The passages he quoted were meant to do a number of things. Condemn me but save me, for starters. Praise my father for following Scripture but condemn him for challenging its authority. Preserve the community. The men in that room – men whose homes had once been opened to my father; men who, like my father, had exchanged their lives for the life of an Apostolic Child of Belief – knew the recited passages and were by then sophisticated enough in Arthur Backstrom's use of Scripture to absorb these shifting messages. No one, I believed then and believe today, misunderstood what was being demanded.

All that long night we received visitors to 309. The Hillmans kept out of the way and quiet; the room would soon be theirs alone. "Who gave you that newspaper?" was the only thing Randy Hillman said, and he said it softly, bravely. It had been Roxy Martin, my old neighbor and baseball pal. She had been out one midnight – without her parents' knowledge, surely – to watch the Ackbees roam. I spotted her behind Jackson's Cafe and we fell into conversation. From the dumpsters Roxy retrieved the day's discarded paper and pointed out the changes, since my father had moved us to the Dahl, in the American and National League standings. Arthur Backstrom never contended that baseball was a sin, but it wasn't just the sports section Roxy Martin gave me. All the news of the state and country and world was in that newspaper, and I brought it home and kept it under my cot with my other possessions.

At twenty-five or thirty or even thirty-five the world is before a man and a life can be built. My father was forty-three. We left both Arthur Backstrom and Syfer and during the next six years, the final third of my life at home, more moves and jobs followed. Nothing of Arthur Backstrom or the Ackbees was ever invoked. The meaning of those months, how to shape them, wasn't addressed, either. What had been the true disaster: our conversion? my disobedience? our departure? Large spans of silence marked those years after we left. My mother said once – we were eating a meal, and it's difficult to imagine how the subject could have arisen – that we had our concerns and God of course has His. But I don't recall if anything more was said.

When I fly over the prairies – it has happened too often to number, the years having brought me to the age my parents were then – I'm still held by their vastness, the mulish towns here and there clinging to abandoned rails like beads of water to a snagged and taut trout line. Each little kingdom keeps its distance, held apart by forces similar to those that keep the planets from ever meeting. The Ackbees – who remembers them now? – are long scattered. They flared before collapse, and in their momentary brilliance consumed all the lesser bodies in proximity. It could have happened in any of a thousand unredeemed towns. Each had its abandoned Dahl, its long box of a hotel constructed during the pioneer days of mudholes and planked sidewalks, the glory gone with an earlier age. Each had its isolation and bewilderment and Bibles. Each had its plumber.

"All these years," I said to my mother, "and he still acts as though it could have been anyone but him who found that newspaper and turned it over to Backstrom." I said this over the telephone on what we both knew would be her last birthday. Speaking Arthur Backstrom's name – or my father's, for that matter – was breaking an implicit taboo. "Does he?" my mother said. "Luke, what can it matter now?" The same water, I once heard her say, has lasted us the life of the world, but rain is only rain for its very short fall. It is neither vicious nor melodramatic to say that Arthur Backstrom destroyed my father. Yet there was nothing he believed with which my father disagreed.

Welcome to My World

He was never able to name the date. It had just . . . begun. Spotty nights of bad sleep had become more frequent, eventually stringing into a week that spilled into a second week, extended into the next month, consumed the winter's entirety. Imagine that each night is a TV show, he told Ingrid, where instead of clumping the commercials, they decide to space them evenly, a thirty-second image of acquisition interjecting itself every minute or two. It would make the show untenable, no? Well, Allman said, welcome to my world.

"So what do the commercials represent?"

"Interrupted sleep. Periods of restlessness."

"That happens to everyone," Ingrid said. "We all have our share of time staring at the ceiling."

"That's not what I'm talking about. I never lie awake. I'm asleep within a minute of eleven, every night. An hour or two are blissful. And then something awakens me. Something tells me to stop sleeping."

Ingrid said nothing. Something about the way her husband described the problem — the personification, his willingness to allow it a voice – gave her a look of worry.

"So I settle back in and ten minutes later it happens again. By six I'm so disgusted, it's a relief to get out of bed."

"Maybe," Ingrid said after awhile, "we need a new alarm clock. One you won't worry will fail."

"Now you're on the right track. I sleep like it's the night before an early job interview and I've got an unreliable alarm clock."

"OK then."

"But our alarm clock's fine. So was the one I replaced last month."

No one at school had an inkling. Allman arrived on time and taught devotedly. No complaints, no missed days, no dozing off before the students' very eyes. There was a grimness about him at times, but of course there was a grimness. How could a twenty-year teacher of high school students not be grim?

"Have you ever thought through the folly of space exploration?" Allman asked John Hoyer, the biology teacher, in the faculty lounge. "The very thing we're looking for, life, a single drop of water, will likely carry the virus that will kill us all. We'll bring back to Earth the seed of our own destruction. There's not much to do when you've come face to face with a virus from Mars."

"Have you been dipping into the science fiction again, Walter?"

"Maybe I have. Maybe I need someone who majored in left brain to tell me it couldn't possibly happen."

"Couldn't *possibly* happen? Who could ever say that, that it couldn't *possibly* happen?"

Which was the problem. In Allman's world, everything was possible.

* * *

For the longest time Allman told no one but Ingrid. Who would understand? Allman didn't need the advice he would surely have received. He couldn't cut back on caffeine – coffee, soda, and chocolate had never played much of a role in his diet. He didn't often drink. He never smoked and had no weight to lose. He exercised daily.

"Teaching can be stressful," was Ingrid's diagnosis.

"Grading all those papers?" Allman said doubtfully.

"You tell me. Is that the part that's most stressful? What about just having to put up with everything? Kids on one side, administration on the other . . . ."

Well, Allman thought, sure. Over the years he had composed for Ingrid – who was *not* a teacher – a long list of complaints. But Allman couldn't fairly say the complaints amounted to much more than aggravations. Stress? His job was secure. It had its rewards. The governor had said teachers were the custodians of our common culture. No, he should not have winked when he said it. But Allman enjoyed the embattled camaraderie this had created in the faculty lounge. Teaching was not at the root of Allman's new problem.

Nor was money. Ingrid coordinated buying for the eight Phelps stores. She had done this since Alex was born – fifteen years now – and the pay was good. Ingrid herself had nothing to do with Allman's predicament, either; their evaluation of one another had changed little in two decades of marriage. And Alex also escaped blame: she had emerged from the rocky years and was now cheerful, energetic, self-sufficient. Allman's search for a diagnosis would need to look elsewhere, and did. He reflected upon his diet; but experimental additions and subtractions had no effect. He became suspicious of the cat; but a late winter ice fishing trip took Allman north for a long weekend, and his nights at Sigurd's Cabins were as miserable as his nights at home. He thought about the furnace, radon levels, the new shampoo Alex had seen on television and brought home. All culprits were investigated thoroughly and cleared.

So there was really nothing to tell. Everything that could be said could be fit into one sentence: Allman couldn't rest – "The engine won't stop racing," is one of the descriptions he gave Ingrid – and there was no reason. John Hoyer was Allman's closest friend, but Allman told him nothing. "You don't begin a story," he said to Ingrid, "if you've got no ending for it."

Ingrid nodded, unconvinced.

"You don't begin a joke that has no punch line."

But what if there were a punch line and Hoyer – or anyone, for that matter – knew it? This was the other reason Allman kept silent. This was what kept him from the doctors. His ailment might be recognized. Maybe a fundamental mechanism was breaking down. Perhaps the great rhythm that governs a life was separating itself from that life. In Allman's trombone-playing days the school band had ground to a halt – during a concert, no less – when the girl playing the triangle had slipped an echo of a beat behind and then, her doggedness approaching panic, run right through the odd 3/4 measure. It had happened almost three decades earlier, but the memory now reappeared to Allman two and three times each day.

Fear was the common thread, Allman realized. Being afraid of this new thing that gripped him, but also afraid of confronting that thing – Allman understood that he was being scared by fear. A strange idea, being afraid of fear. Like falling in love with love, Allman mused, or being unhappy with unhappiness. Sleep problems could be tamed, Allman supposed. But fear, having broke into full gallop, would run and run forever.

Allman found a peculiar consolation. He and Ingrid and Alex lived on the edge of a great slough that wound behind their yard and then along the county road that led into town. Daily the inhabitants would venture out: weasels in winter, geese against the layered autumn sky, rabbits appearing almost every day of the year. Allman stood at the back window, often for large blocks of each late afternoon, and watched. An imaginary wall kept the animals from coming too close, an invisible cushion prevented the birds from dropping too low. Could they sense a change in atmosphere, Allman wondered, when they came too near the houses? Was there a field of human anxiety that caused, perhaps, a high-pitched warning? The deer especially entranced Allman. They entered the yard quickly but gracefully on their walking-stick legs, bounding up from the swamp like bubbles rising from heated water.

"Your pets," Ingrid commented. She was amused, and somewhat comforted, by the power the deer held over her husband. "There's calm about them, isn't there? Those deep black eyes, and never a sound."

But weeks of observation had disabused Allman of such an idea. Those deep eyes darted. The noses twitched and the slightest provocation – a breeze, maybe, or the whine of a truck as it slowed for town – gave the deer a start. Often Allman could only wonder what the provocation was. What frightened the deer away was frequently undetectable.

* * *

He became susceptible to metaphor. "When *you* dive into the pool," he wanted to say, "you swim along the bottom all the way to the other side. But my dives are shallow, as though I'm fitted into a life jacket that keeps me from getting below the surface. I'm fighting horseflies off my shoulders all night long."

Wanted to say, but didn't, because Ingrid had probably heard enough. Had she been less tolerant, she might have suggested that Allman had become self-absorbed, obsessed; and possibly this obsession was the fuel that sustained the dysfunction. Allman understood this. But something had happened to him – was *still* happening to him – and he could conceive of no cure that didn't involve first identifying the source.

"Do you dream much?" he asked John Hoyer.

"World peace, that sort of thing?"

"I'm being literal. Real dreams: close your eyes and make your own movie."

Hoyer, seated in the corner of the lounge, thought a moment. "I guess I don't, that I remember. Certainly not like we all used to. But I suppose *you* do, if you're asking."

"Always."

"And you remember these dreams?"

"Yes, and they're almost uniformly bad. Nightmares."

One dream involved a van. Allman was back visiting a place stipulated by the logic of dreams to be the town he had grown up in, though the setting looked like nothing Allman had ever seen. Throughout the long dream Allman felt an anxiety: he needed to end this visit and return to his home. But there was always a reason not to leave, some new person to talk to or memory to recall. When he finally left he ignored Ingrid's advice – she was in the passenger seat; Alex wasn't in the van, not yet – and took a back road instead of the freeway. This back road was under construction, loose and unreliable. Allman took the road because it passed near something he wanted to see, an object never named in the dream. But the road ran in large circles and Allman passed a grader once, a second time, then a third time, and with each pass the road became more treacherous. Allman gave the grader a wide berth on his third pass and got stuck in deep mud. He felt the van sink, and though he waited at the steering wheel for the sinking to end, it continued, then accelerated, the mud reaching over the tires and climbing the sides of the van, which had now become a school bus. The rear of the bus dropped deep into the thick brown mud, tipping Allman and Ingrid back as though they were astronauts preparing for lift-off. By now it was apparent there would be no escape. Allman scrambled out of his driver's seat as the bus became darker. The mud ran up the side windows rapidly – as it reached the windshield Allman said something intended to reassure Ingrid and Alex, who was now suddenly in this jam with them. But he knew there was no hope. The mud spread over the windshield, the circle of daylight diminishing until there was nothing but darkness.

"Awful," Hoyer said, looking genuinely horrified. "Where in the world did that come from?"

Where indeed, Allman thought. Hoyer had asked the relevant question.

A second dream was disturbing in a different way. In this dream it was Alex's wedding day. She was still fifteen, which seemed not to matter, and she was frantic. She pleaded with both Allman and Ingrid, who acted like Golden Age of Television parents, smiling and reassuring her. Gradually they sent Alex off to the ceremony, then settled into other things, forgetting their daughter and the wedding in a way that can only occur in dreams. And then, long chapters of dreaming later, Alex suddenly reappeared to Allman – Ingrid had left the dream – and was hysterical. She had driven all the way back from the church, which had been locked. Allman should have given her the keys. Where were the keys? But Allman knew nothing about any keys.

Allman clicked through the Internet as though poking for a ball lost among leaves. Dream analysis sites abounded. The varieties of dreams were impressive: there were the familiar Falling Dreams, Pursuit Dreams, Late for an Appointment Dreams, Test Day Dreams, but also Bird Dreams, Insect Dreams, even Farting Dreams. There was the Dream of the Great Frog. Of course there was no Dream of the Sinking Bus, but Allman found a Quicksand Dream, even a Lost the Keys Dream. The interpretations Allman studied fell into two categories. Some were, paradoxically, cryptic and obvious both. "Events are crowding around you" was the interpretation one might give to the bus dream. But what events? And why were they crowding? But even these explanations were more satisfying than those that read like horoscope parodies, or mutual fund commercials. "You acknowledge being presented with myriad opportunities for growth," read the interpretation of the Imprisoning a Loved

One Dream. "Your challenge is now to release those you love to pursue their dreams." But of course, Allman muttered.

"I don't know much about dream interpretation," Hoyer said. "Some of that stuff you're reading might be guesswork."

The point wasn't what the dreams might mean, anyway. The point, Allman decided, was that he wouldn't be dreaming these dreams were his nights something other than – another favorite metaphor – a walk through a Halloween haunted house, the kind where you pay a few dollars and then wind your way from room to room, ghouls popping up at every turn, and soon there's no difference between the ghouls appearing and the ghouls not appearing, the anxiety burning at one constant temperature and the heat producing these ridiculous images, crying daughters and mud pits. *That's* the problem, he told Hoyer, and in that way he told Hoyer everything, the words escaping from Allman like mourning doves from a barn in flames.

* * *

There was no end to the search for clues, the analysis. Even after Allman told himself to simply accept this new condition, to stop the questioning – on hopeful days he understood that acceptance wouldn't be surrender, but rather something that might allow him to transcend dysfunction – even then, another possibility would suggest itself. Current events, for example. The airwaves were filled with speculation: passenger planes as missiles, poisoned food supplies, contaminated ventilation systems, nuclear briefcases, all supplementing the old terrors of plane crashes, hotel fires, political assassinations. Allman noted that over the past several years he had relied heavily on his radio, falling into the habit of listening to the news as the last thing he did before falling asleep and the first thing upon awakening. Occasionally during the long half-conscious nights – 1:59, 2:59, 3:59 – he had switched on the radio to hear the hour's headlines. Catastrophe could happen anytime and reassurance was available by merely pushing a button. It was that easy to know. But rest, Allman recognized, was difficult in such a world.

"There are two types of people," Hoyer liked to say. "Those who finish their thoughts." Which was clever, Allman acknowledged, but, more importantly, understated. Allman said so: "John, we've evolved to the point where *none* of us is able to finish his thoughts. So what's this nonsense about there being *two* types of people?"

Evolved, used by a layperson, especially an English teacher, made John Hoyer feisty. "What do you know about it?"

"Quite a lot, I think." Allman had assigned his classes *The Natural*, and after they had read the book Allman brought in the film. He hadn't seen it in twenty years or more, when it had been in the theaters, a big commercial hit. "When I asked the kids what they thought, John, they all said the movie was good but slow. And they were right. I was amazed at how *ponderous* that film is. It never seemed that way when it came out."

The point, to Allman, was that *The Natural* was but one more piece of evidence of acceleration. Movies that once seemed to accurately portray the pace of life, the *feel* of life, now reflected a slow motion civilization Allman could hardly believe had ever included him. But it had. One college summer Allman had taken a month of long afternoons to read *War and Peace*, all fourteen hundred pages, deriving pleasure from, among all the other things, the shifting of chapters from right hand to left, like sand falling through an hourglass. In those years poverty had forced on Allman a rule that kept him from buying a book so long as any other book he owned remained unread. Possibly the cover-to-cover reading of so many books, many of them bad books, hadn't been helpful; but now Allman purchased stacks of books and understood, even as he left the store, that many would never be read. Even those he did read cooled after two or three chapters, unable to compete with the allure of this or that book left on the store shelf.

And it was not only Allman. Who didn't exhibit the same impatience? Allman once prided himself on a nuanced use of language, subtle arguments, a craftsmanship evident in the reports he circulated as the faculty's union rep. Were these reports read? Allman guessed not – the questions answered in his memos were asked days later by the new social studies teacher, the band director, even venerable Mrs. Walker. Over the years Allman's three-page reports became one-page reports. They conformed to a five-paragraph pattern, the central points leading and finishing each paragraph and often set in a bold type that reminded Allman of Braille. "You've put away the scalpel . . ." is how Hoyer described the change, allowing Allman to reply, as if scripted, ". . . and replaced it with my chainsaw."

The chainsaw was necessary because nothing less could attract attention. A state of agitation had descended upon the entire culture. Would the other fundamentals – eating, drinking, breathing itself – go the way of sleep? What, Allman wondered, was next?

* * *

In April Alex was inducted into the Honor Society. Allman and Ingrid took pictures on the soft brown lawn and then the three of them joined two hundred others – a few dozen students and their parents, siblings, teachers, assorted aunts, uncles, and grandparents – at a banquet in the school cafeteria. The speaker, an education professor from the state college, offered his congratulations and, after apologizing for the indulgence, his humble look toward the future. A heavy rain fell on the drive home. The evening extended to midnight with a reception for neighbors and Alex's friends. Allman moved from the front door to the kitchen to the punch bowl, snapping the camera now and then, exhausted and enjoying, from a distance, his daughter.

He went to bed near one o'clock and slept soundly for an hour before beginning to turn, at intervals, from side to side. Allman was aware of an intense pleasure each time he settled into a new position, the pleasure of rest as escape, as though he had slipped below life's traffic. But the stillness was only preparation for a sudden release of energy, a jerk that Allman understood, as hour passed hour, had become his essence. The quiet was only temporary, a prelude. A great law had inverted itself. Allman walked into the dark living room and lowered himself into a chair, allowing his eyes to comprehend the shape of the furniture, a bouquet of balloons, boxes on the coffee table. He heard a sudden rustling at his feet: a tightly crumpled ball of discarded wrapping paper was opening, even after half the night. Another hemisphere of that balled paper would push itself out in a few more hours, inevitably. Allman began to softly cry. He cradled his head in the palms of his hands and watched the contorted paper turn a few restless degrees and he began to tremble.

In the morning he spoke with Dr. Stevenson's nurse. Why had he waited so long? Even in dreaming he knew he should have made the visit: a few weeks earlier a woman in white, unrecognizable to Allman, had watched him gravely and said, "I'm very worried about you, Walter." Then she had opened a large book to a full-page photograph, glossy and colorful, that seemed to show a magnified flower, or perhaps flares rising from the surface of the sun. "What you have is Phelps Disease." *Phelps*: the word had been a gift, spoken with such assurance by the dream doctor that Allman woke happy, certain a truth had been revealed. But when he asked the computer about Phelps Disease he received no answer. Phelps, a common enough name in Allman's part of the state, apparently held no medical significance.

He was able to negotiate an immediate appointment. The examination was thorough – lights were shown here and there and the many questions gave Allman the opportunity to talk and talk. Dr. Stevenson – a woman, though not the doctor his dream had created – appeared puzzled, possibly too tolerant. Allman did not want to inspire tolerance. But there were categories of sleep disorders, all of which Allman seemed to elude. He was prescribed a single pill, chalky white and hardly larger than a watch battery, to be swallowed each night.

Can the body produce caffeine? Allman had asked. Antihistamines? What did his doctor think about things like hypnosis or meditation? Allman's enthusiasm – the middle-of-the-night despair still lingered and fueled the urgency in his questions – seemed to push Dr. Stevenson toward caution. "Reducing stress is always a good thing," she said.

Allman purchased compact discs. There were nine of them, *The Foundations of Meditation,* and he listened while driving to and from school. The idea of a still mind was attractive, though there was baggage, of course. "Lift the corners of the mouth to bring to the lips a slight smile," instructed the laid-back, vaguely medical voice that accompanied Allman as he passed the liquor stores and overhead wires, sprawling fields of canopied gas pumps, proliferating billboards. "Sigh deeply for no apparent reason. Weep without unhappiness. Cultivate a distaste for milk and eggs." In the hour before Ingrid arrived home – the hour for watching deer, previously – Allman practiced. He sat on a folding chair, eyes closed, and worked hard at ceasing to think. Weeks passed and he seemed to progress – a change was occurring, though whether by meditation or prescription or something else, or nothing at all, was difficult to determine. And there were frequent relapses.

Where would all of this lead? Perhaps Allman's restlessness, clutter, imbalance – that, too, was part of the suffering: there wasn't even a name for what he was experiencing – perhaps this was a lasting condition, but Allman refused to believe it. Sometimes the silliness shamed him. Those who had real problems would never be able to understand Allman's unhappiness. Were *he* ever to be struck by tragedy, this sleep problem, Allman was certain, would evaporate. He imagined a deer bounding into the oncoming lane, causing an approaching semitrailer to brake and swerve, large sheets of snow flying from the truck roof like plywood in the wind, followed by long and delicate maneuvers to extricate Allman from the wreckage, his secondhand Saturn crumpled as Alex's wrapping paper, the meditation disc continuing to spin and play the way radios continued with Their Song in those fifties teenage crash movies, Allman himself in and out of consciousness through the chaos of the emergency room, Ingrid and Alex arriving and conferring with the surgeon. And during all of this, Allman imagined, he would be experiencing a profound calm, so that when Ingrid fretted that he might have fallen asleep at the wheel, mentioning to the doctor his sleep problems and causing the doctor to turn inquiringly down toward him, Allman would be able to look his surgeon in the eye and say, with utter serenity, "It was never anything. All of that is behind me now."

* * *

One school year ended and another began. Winter arrived early and emphatically, a thick snowfall darkening the Great Lakes the entire second week of November. School was delayed two hours on Tuesday, and when Allman arrived he found John

Hoyer gingerly unwinding a long scarf studded with marbles of ice; neither had heard the radio announcement until already in their cars, and they had the lounge to themselves.

"Are you ready for this?" asked Allman. "The next five months?"

The ice rattled off Hoyer's wool scarf like lights being unwound from a Christmas tree, Hoyer moving cautiously to keep the wet beads from dropping down his neck. "My guess is that you are suspicious about such an abrupt beginning. Maybe Earth has tilted from its axis and the government is refusing to tell anyone?"

Allman looked into his coffee and considered the possibility. It wasn't as farfetched as other things he had believed. It wasn't, at any rate, impossible; anyone had the freedom to believe or disbelieve, but honesty forced you to acknowledge that few things were impossible. "You know what the biggest government secret is, don't you?" Not until the words were out did Allman understand that he was speaking only to provoke a reaction. He was playing.

"How many years ago was it, John, when some astronomers announced they had discovered an asteroid on line for a direct hit? Big enough to split Earth in two. I remember the year of impact was calculated to be 2036, because I remember thinking I'd be seventy-five years old. It was the biggest news of our age – the biggest news in the history of the planet, if people had the capacity to accept it. But then the next day, the *very next day*, it was all retracted. A mistake had been made, the government said, some measurement had been misrecorded. The asteroid would miss us by a million miles and we could all go back to whatever we were worrying about before we had been told about the asteroid in the first place. Do you remember all that?"

Hoyer was spreading his scarf on a radiator to dry. "I'd forgotten about it. But sure."

"How plausible," Allman continued, "does that retraction sound? Is it possible that astronomers, with their Ph.D.'s and billion-dollar instruments, could be confident enough about their observations to go public, only to change their minds in twenty-four hours, after causing a tremendous public panic? Is that likely?"

"So there's a secret? There was never an asteroid?"

"There *was* an asteroid, and still is. But there's nothing to do about it, and very good reasons not to have panic or fatalism or despair, so the government chose to discredit the whole story. Deny it before any real damage could be done. It's the best explanation for what happened that week."

Hoyer watched Allman closely. "So our days are numbered, and some day in 2036, thirty years from now, is the last number? Is that what you believe?"

Allman kept his eyes fastened to Hoyer's. That was not what he believed. But it had taken this speech, the deceit of this confession, for Allman to discover that he did not believe.

"Well," John Hoyer said after deciding he would not get an answer. "Anything is possible, I suppose." He sat down and looked at the dark splotches the melting snow had administered to his pants legs. "Walter, you told me last spring that you saw a doctor about your sleep problems."

Allman nodded.

"And?"

"A lot of describing, a lot of investigating. She gave me a pill, thinking it might be temporary."

Hoyer ran a hand through his beard and leaned forward unhappily. Allman's attention was drawn to the rings of skin that cushioned Hoyer's eyes, eyes that now vaguely resembled small browning fruit settled in among beds of lettuce. "All these things you've described for me, Walter, this past year – you've been accurate as hell. The flipping around like a fish in the boat, those damn dreams, the tenacity of it all – that's just exactly how it is."

"Since when?"

Hoyer shrugged. "Who knows when these things start?"

"Well," said Allman – too quickly, not having reasoned out a reply. "See a doctor, I guess."

"That helped you? The medicine – has it caused an improvement?"

Improvement. Allman closed his eyes to defend against interruption and began to recreate his nights – not all of them restful, of course, but some restful, here and there, a far cry from those dark days of the previous spring.

"Sure," he said, looking at Hoyer again. "There's been an improvement."

Hoyer, in spite of himself, brightened somewhat. "You're back to where you were before?" he asked greedily.

"Before?" Allman closed his eyes once again, this time to imagine the world that had existed prior to the undefined beginning of his sufferings. The characteristics of sleep – it was not something he had ever thought of then. Nights then were like nights now, he supposed, like the good ones now. Not that they had been perfect. That didn't seem probable. But bad nights had been bad in a different way, he guessed.

Hoyer waited patiently for his answer. When Allman finally opened his eyes it was with a smile that masked the failure. "Before, John?" He said no more. Before had lost its meaning.

Farm Buying

It was a curious little town, Jonathan thought, the town to which the Amundson farm belonged. The inhabitants were poor but hated the poor and their claim on handouts. Relatively affluent cousins who lived in the city were pitied and mocked for a supposed ineptitude. The city itself was despised for not only its multitudes, but also its crime, yet it was the local criminals – drunken ruffians, mostly, or meth lab proprietors – and not the sheriff's men who enjoyed the home crowd's support. And television was cherished because it made those multitudes and their otherness familiar and so allowed you to laugh with the laugh track and luxuriate in imagined tolerance. Jonathan observed all of these traits in his girlfriend's older brother Tim, who was at this moment launching a toy football toward the cat.

Christmas Day. Jonathan had arrived with Jodi at her parents' home shortly after breakfast, while the roads were still empty and the frost hadn't yet burned off the trees. Now, toward noon, family were beginning to arrive. Jonathan had prepared for this with memorized note cards, but it was quickly apparent that the effort had been futile. Jodi's eight brothers and sisters, all older, had been born in each of four decades. All but Tim were married. Carol, the oldest, now well into middle age, had been married twice and even had a daughter who was married. Between the siblings and their spouses there was an overabundance of *J*s – Jodi, of course, and John, John, Jimmy, Jake, Joan, Joe, and Jo, who was sometimes called Mary Jo and sometimes Mary, which caused confusion with one of the Johns' wife Mary (Joe was also married to a Mary) – and there were also nicknames. There were the Konfusing *K*s, as

Jodi called them (Jodi's wink convinced Jonathan she meant *confusing* to be spelled alliteratively): Kristin, Kjersten, and Kirsten. And Nicklaus and Michael, Danielle and Megan, all the grandchildren. Jodi had painstakingly given Jonathan all of the information – there was a Stacy and a Staci, she warned, and a Theodore who was never called Ted and a Ted who always was – but even she had difficulty remembering which was the girl, Taylor or Jep.

They arrived in waves, their cars stretching far down the long farm driveway. The masses of humanity pushed Jonathan from the living room, already crowded by a generous Christmas tree, to the dining room, where an ancient oak table whose history could be divined through its cuts and bruises was encircled by a constellation of card tables and folding chairs; to the plywood-paneled rec room, its empty bookshelves and odd assortment of furniture in servitude to a mammoth and elevated television screen; and finally to the kitchen, where Jodi's mother, quite close to seventy, was heroically constructing Christmas dinner. "Something smells good," Jonathan offered, meaning the turkey.

"Who are you?" asked a woman wearing a breathtaking tower of blonde hair. She was one of a number of daughters or daughters-in-law or both now entering the room.

"Well, Hillary, this is Jonathan, of course," came a reply. This from a woman perhaps ten years Jonathan's senior. *Jonathan* was given emphasis to highlight its exoticism. "He's Jodi's."

"*Jodi's,*" two or three of the women responded knowingly. As they processed this information their voices rode a long incline up and then over a worn hill of well-intentioned condescension. Did they not think he could see their smiles and winks? Did one of them really have a setting of holly and ivy painted on her forehead?

"Or she's mine," Jonathan said. "Depends on how you look at it."

Hillary's face went blank with a harmless irritability.

"You're in enemy territory on Christmas. Outnumbered a skadillion to one. I'd say she's the one who has captured you."

By now young children had reached the kitchen, the first charge of little Columbuses swarming into their grandmother's ordered world. Jodi's mother broke from cooking long enough to greet her grandchildren and admire the toys they had unwrapped at their homes the previous night. Many of these toys depended on a familiarity with technology and popular culture that Mrs. Amundson could not claim. To her this only made the gifts more wondrous. "Isn't that something!" she exclaimed. "Will you look at that!"

"So, Jonathan." Holly and Ivy, now. Name tags, Jonathan would have to tell Jodi, would have been a good idea. "I hear you're a computer boy."

There were so many points of interest in that one sentence. *I hear*: Jonathan would need to accustom himself to the fact that vast tides of speculation had already washed from one family member to another. *Computer*: better to leave that idea untouched – nothing would be gained by pushing into the intricacies of software development. *Boy*: it was inevitable that anyone brought home by Jodi, who was less than a year out of college and younger than her oldest niece, would be a novelty. Jonathan was certain he would be able to establish himself as something other than merely young. If that would be wise.

"Computers?" said Hillary. "Have you talked to Tim about that?" She looked, Jonathan marveled, like a compass swung open, her head the fulcrum and her pile of hair one of the legs. Jonathan attempted to remember what Jodi had said about her. Could she be the sister with the string of rushed and broken romances? All of them doomed from the start, Jodi had said, a clear example of trying to pound a round peg into a square hole.

"As a matter of fact, I have."

"We all knew you and Tim would get along famously," said Holly. Which could have meant anything. Even without the tenuous computer connection – Tim, sometimes a mechanic, had taken a course at the tech college over in Daw to learn about car engine computers; an amazing coincidence, one of the sisters had told Jodi – Jonathan had sensed that Jodi's brother was someone he needed to know well. He was a power broker in the Amundson family. Tim, four years older than Jodi and therefore roughly Jonathan's age, had been the only Amundson to stay home. He supervised the farm – now a hobby farm, more or less – and was his parents' representative, even their guardian, one might say. His staying had allowed all those others their distance.

They had met twice before, Jonathan and Tim. On Thanksgiving Friday Jodi had convinced Tim to drive down to her apartment in the city for a party. Tim had clearly been uneasy, Jonathan observed, so deep inside the beltway and expected to interact with people about whose histories he hadn't a clue. Tim had said nothing when introduced to Jonathan, whose name and dress (collarless shirt; glasses with smallish and untinted lenses) struck him as outlandish, even effete. There were eight or ten others there, Jodi's school friends and their guys, none wearing denim jackets or boots. Bowling league, crops, which young cop was sleeping with which young teacher – all the usual topics of conversation were suddenly unavailable. Tim had left early. He later told Jodi it had felt like his class reunion, a good idea until hijacked by the college kids.

And then Tim and Jonathan had met that morning, Christmas morning. The morning after the angels' appearance. To have a whole day at the farm Jodi had set the alarm for six o'clock. She and Jonathan had loaded a few presents into the Mesa Climber and there had been an awkward moment when Jonathan produced, from the back of the refrigerator, a cabernet dressed in a super-sized Christmas bow. "No, silly," Jodi had said. "This isn't the movies." William and Helen Amundson had lived at the farm forty-six and sixty-eight years, respectively, and were in no need of a house-warming gift. Their faith, as interpreted by their generation, forbid alcohol, on Christmas most of all. So Jodi and her guest arrived at the farm, after a ninety-minute drive, without the bottle. Tim heard their engine and was the first to the door. "Season's greetings!" Jonathan said heartily. Tim, with a ferocity that may or may not have been playful, put both hands on Jonathan's chest and shoved him backwards into the snow.

"Did I hear my name?" Tim now bellowed. If so, it was with the ears of a deer – Jonathan estimated there were upwards of fifty people balled into what was only a modest-sized farmhouse. The voice arrived fifteen seconds before Tim was able to push his way through to where Jonathan and his interrogator were standing. Straight out of central casting, as Jonathan had decided that morning: six foot two, flannel shirt with top buttons open to reveal a T-shirt bearing the logo of a truck manufacturer, an odd whisker here and there on the chin, a healing cut on an ear lobe. Earlier in the week Jonathan had read a *Wall Street Journal* article on a Dozen Dead End Careers; it occurred to him now that Tim was pursuing a handful – television repair, automobile cassette deck installation, freelance logging – simultaneously. "Jonathan!" Tim had said loudly. As though making a discovery. "Jonathan –" he paused to make certain of the mispronunciation – "Flaherty? Isn't it? Do you like to Flahert a lot with the girls?" As witless as Jonathan had heard since high school, but the volume swept away any possibility of a cogent or even audible response.

"Tim," Holly said in a reprimand camouflaging amusement. Tim was bouncing his gaze between her and Hillary, basking in appreciation. Jonathan glanced up as a precaution against falling hair. "You two!" Holly continued. "Didn't I say they'd hit it off famously?"

To which Hillary's eyes narrowed. "Do you like football?" Holly nodded vigorously at the question's relevance.

"You should know that about Tim," she shouted toward Jonathan. "He's an enormous college football fan. What big game is there today, Tim? There must be something."

"Tennessee and West Virginia." Spoken with a whiff of disdain at having to educate the masses. "It's already under way."

"On Christmas Day, for crying out loud," protested Hillary. "I hate that."

"It's an important game, though," Jonathan said with an earnest smile. This was ground he could compete on. "It's the first bowl game of the holidays."

Ignoring him, Hillary bore her eyes into Tim. "Don't you *dare* ruin Mom's Christmas by getting everyone to end up around the television over some stupid football game." There was genuine anger in her voice. There was history.

The muscles in Tim's face tightened. "I'll worry about the game," he said, speaking at half speed for emphasis. "You just try to get through the day without losing those clothes." Another reference, Jonathan gathered, to history.

* * *

Jodi led Jonathan to the rec room and directed him to a niece, the oldest daughter of her second-oldest brother. "Ashley?" the girl said in tentative introduction. She was a high school junior and captain of her volleyball team. She was hoping to one day major in computer science. Ashley? served computer career questions toward Jonathan and he glanced intermittently at the bright and loud television screen above them. The game was nearing halftime. West Virginia led, 6-3.

A crowd began to collect between the television and a small table bearing peanuts, pretzels, and ginger ale. "We're all multi-taskers," Jonathan heard from over his shoulder. The voice seemed to belong to Marilyn, who was either the wife of a brother or a stray cousin or someone not named Marilyn at all. "It's boring to talk without a television on." She laughed as she said this but, Jonathan noticed, it was indeed the case that the people most at ease were those eating, talking, and watching the football game, all at more or less the same time. "Do people in computers get a lot of time off?" As Jonathan considered the question he overheard one of the Johns: "Wrapping paper is like magnets with these cats." Additional breezes of conversation wafted through the room. A woman was concerned about her child's floating feces. Someone wondered about Santa Claus and idolatry. Jonathan heard a pleasurable snort from Tim and glanced up to see a commercial in which an icy wet bottle of beer was superimposed beneath a cheerleader doing the splits. "Honestly," said Marilyn, her voice rising from annoyance toward disgust. "These sports commercials have set the cause of women's rights back twenty goddamn years."

"How many years?" asked Tim gleefully. Consternation froze Ashley?'s face, and she began to back from the room. Most everyone else rotated toward a corner rocking chair and its occupant, Jodi's father. Marilyn's words seemed to drop away until the only one remaining was *goddamn*. Echoing in spite of shag carpet.

"Well," said Mr. Amundson. He looked down thoughtfully. "Well."

"Do we really need football on Christmas Day?" said Jodi.

"Gol darn right we do," said Tim, watching Marilyn. "I've got twenty bucks riding on this game."

"He probably does," Jonathan heard from a woman ladling ginger ale into a plastic cup. Mary? Karen? Karen. Her eyes caught Jonathan's.

"Of course I do," said Tim. But with a shadow of

discomfort. Jonathan watched as Tim flashed a vulnerable glance toward his father. "Go, Tennessee!" This was a concluding statement of principle. Tim brushed past Karen on his way out of the room, giving her a sneer that struck Jonathan as being, in large measure, affectionate.

Karen, carefully balancing her ginger ale, stepped closer to Jonathan and Jodi. She had a pretty face, long blonde hair that snapped with winter's static electricity, and a voice half an octave lower than Jonathan's unconscious expectation. By now a sense of equilibrium had returned to the room. Pre-*goddamn* levels of eating, talking, and football watching established themselves. Mr. Amundson was again gently rocking, surveying with contentment the multitudes his life on the farm had yielded.

"There's no greater culture shock," said Karen, "than a return home. After all these years you'd think we'd get used to it. Aren't I right, Jodi?"

Jodi shrugged. "You've been away fifteen years longer than I have."

"You've got to feel for Tim," Karen continued. Speaking to Jodi and Jonathan as a couple, which Jonathan appreciated. "How easy can it be to live in two eras at once? You forget, now that we've got our own lives, what kind of world we grew up in." She turned toward Jonathan directly. "Has Jodi told you? No school dances. No cheerleading for us girls. That was dancing. No smoking or alcohol, obviously. That went without saying. No movies. Can you believe that? We couldn't even go into town to see a movie."

"I went to movies," said Jodi.

"An advantage of being the last child, no doubt. But the old ideas of what kept you out of hell didn't change soon enough for my generation."

"Tim seems to be in good graces," ventured Jonathan. It was difficult to imagine him constricted by the rules Karen had, after two decades or more, recited flawlessly.

"Oh, Mom and Dad love him. You look at the world differently when you're no longer responsible for your children, I suppose."

"It's more like he's responsible for them," said Jodi.

Karen looked into her ginger ale. "I can't believe I tried to fan the flames when Tim said he had a bet riding on this stupid game. Still jockeying to be in better graces with the folks, is what it was. Old habits die hard." She glanced up sheepishly. "I mean, who cares? All over Tennessee versus . . . ."

"West Virginia," said Jonathan. "I bet on it, too."

"You, too? *Guys,*" she said in mock disgust.

"But it's not really betting," said Jodi. "You don't even care who wins, do you? It's some office numbers game you're in."

"A grid."

"Oh, a grid," Karen smiled as she turned toward the television. "That's different. Anyone can lose twenty dollars on a bet. But *my* future brother-in-law –"

"Karen," Jodi said in reprimand; that she and Jonathan would marry was probable but not certain.

"— loses his money on grids."

Jonathan could hear a general commotion from the dining room. Dinner would soon be ready, seemed the general feeling. Karen excused herself and the seven or eight other Amundsons in the rec room began to reluctantly pull away from the television. Jonathan had been noticing strange proceedings on the screen. There had been a failed extra point and then a safety, resulting in an improbable 12-5 score. The ball was now mired hopelessly in the middle of the field and the half's final seconds were ticking away. All these people, Jonathan thought. Each one oblivious to the implications.

"Come on," Jodi said. "Dinner can't be long."

"Give me a moment to check something." Jonathan rummaged through a pocket, pausing to pay homage as Mr.

Amundson, the last person to leave save Jodi and Jonathan, passed by. Then Jonathan produced and unfolded two stapled sheets of paper. "These halftime numbers. They're winners for me, I'm pretty sure."

"Just don't study your grid too long. Being late to the table wouldn't be cool."

"Sure," Jonathan said in a voice so detached that Jodi stopped in the doorway and gave an amused smile.

"Okay?"

Jonathan looked up. "Okay."

"That's a nice boy," Jodi said sweetly, then left Jonathan to his numbers.

* * *

"So," Tim said, after an indecent interval following the prayer. "What's this I hear about . . . about . . . well, I guess there's no other way to say it. The grid."

"Eat," said Karen. "God you've a big mouth."

"So says the woman who told us about Jonathan's grid in the first place. Whatever a grid is."

Tim's voice penetrated beyond the dining room table and its leaves and various temporary extensions – beyond, that is, Mr. and Mrs. Amundson, six other couples, including Jodi and her guest, and Tim – and carried to the satellite card tables that had spread into adjoining rooms. The option of ignoring Tim was not available.

"It's nothing more than an assignment of numbers," said Jonathan. Daring Tim to continue on.

"An assignment of numbers." Tim looked around the table for help. There seemed to be little interest; Mr. Amundson asked a daughter-in-law Jonathan didn't remember meeting whether she would like to eat more sweet potatoes.

But a small voice from a card table unknowingly came to Tim's assistance. "What are you guys talking about?" said Michael, who was eight.

"Just numbers," Jonathan said quickly and reassuringly. "Everyone who wants to participate is given numbers for a bowl game. If the one-place digits in the score match your numbers, you win." Jonathan paused. "The more unlikely the score, the more you win."

"What kind of money are we talking about?" said Tim. "It sounds like an easy way to drop a lot of money and fast."

Karen noted the escalation. "Isn't there something better than wagering we can talk about?"

"On Christmas Day," agreed Jodi.

"It's all tied to the number of participants, Tim. We *have* had some pretty big numbers in the past, due to the fact that interests in our grid have been syndicated." Then, for good measure: "There's actually a secondary market for the grid's capital calls. An investment trust, you could say."

"That makes sense," said Mrs. Amundson. She said it absentmindedly, while buttering a dinner roll. Her contribution made Jonathan uneasy; using ridicule to fend off Tim would be easier out of the presence of Jodi's parents. On the other hand, a wave of good fortune was emboldening Jonathan. He was spending Christmas Day with Jodi, whom he was likely to marry. And his halftime numbers were two and five.

"What does all that mean?" said Tim. "Did you put in money on today's game?"

"I did."

"On Tennessee? Or West Virginia. Betting on West Virginia would be dumb."

"The teams are irrelevant. Remember, it's nothing more than an assignment of numbers."

"Syndicated," Jodi added. "An investment trust." Ever

so slightly propping up her brother with this gentle reprimand. Jonathan appreciated this even as he took it as a sign he should begin to work on reconciliation with Tim.

"So," Tim said. "You bet but it doesn't matter who wins."

"Right."

"It only matters what the score is."

"That's right."

Tim looked around the table to gauge reaction. Most everyone seemed interested, if only mildly. More curious than aligned with either Tim or Jonathan. There was some ambivalence, Jonathan sensed, as to whether betting on football was a bad thing.

"Well?" said Tim. "Let's cut to the chase. Are you winning or are you losing?"

"I've done some of both this year. Won a little, lost a little."

"It evens out, doesn't it," said Jodi.

But Tim saw the opening. "How about today? How are you doing on *today's* game?" Swallowing the hook wholly.

"Today? Today I won on the halftime numbers."

Tim betrayed a look of disappointment. To hear Jodi's boy admit a loss would have attracted attention. The Bible didn't admire gambling, was a reason to oppose it. But to lose at gambling, to fritter away money obtained through hard work and good fortune, through whatever computer work had in common with good weather and fair prices, the gamble that was farming, the only acceptable endeavor of chance – for Jonathan to have admitted a loss would have been delicious. Not that Tim wished him anything worse than temporary discomfort.

"Is that right?" Tim asked. "Came up a few dollars on the good side? This time?"

"Thirty-five hundred dollars." Jonathan reached into his pocket to pull out the grid and the sheet of contributors stapled to it. In movies a funny line is followed by a few seconds of emptiness to allow the audience a good laugh before the story starts up again; Jonathan's deliberate unfolding of his papers allowed his audience time to react. Looks were exchanged: sisters looked at their husbands and brothers looked at their wives. The cousins, more inclined than their parents to smile, looked at one another and smiled in wonderment. "Wow!" said Michael.

Jodi's father seemed uncertain as to what had just happened. He looked around the table and smiled tentatively. "Thirty-five dollars," he acknowledged.

"Thirty-five *hundred* dollars, dear." Jodi's mother passed the green beans uneasily.

"You guys play for keeps," said Karen. "How much do you have to bet, invest, whatever, to win three-and-a-half grand?"

"Not that much," Jodi answered quickly. "Because it's syndicated."

"Two hundred dollars," said Jonathan.

"Two hundred dollars!" Mr. Amundson said triumphantly.

Furious mental activity followed. Jodi's family – excepting her parents and the younger grandchildren, many of whom were now giggling at a small marshmallow that had become lodged in one of Taylor's nostrils – each considered the implications of this information about her guest. He spent big. He won big, though the potential for other outcomes was present. What did all this portend for Jodi? was the question. Dishes of Christmas dinner rotated around the tables and the most preliminary of conclusions began to form. Tim's formed first. "Mom," he said, looking across the table and into her eyes. "This is a wonderful meal, but you'll have to excuse me." He rose from his chair, glass of milk in one hand and half-filled plate grasped tightly in the other. "I'll be damned if I'm going to listen to this on Christmas Day."

Tim's outburst was Jonathan's good fortune, Jonathan thought. Disapproval tilted toward Jodi's brother. Tim had retreated to the rec room, where the game's second half was now in progress. He sat sullenly before the television set, eventually eating all of the food he had brought with him and then placing the empty plate directly beneath his chair. Family wandered in once the meal had ended, led by children and then their fathers and next a few mothers.

Jonathan kept to the living room, where he tried to interest a small girl in the lights on the tree. Presents having been opened, however, Christmas was essentially over and childlike wonder dormant for another year. "Do you like the reds best, or the blues?" Jonathan asked from a crouching position beneath the tree. "I don't know," the girl – Melissa, Marissa, Melinda, Mialisa – answered, resolutely refusing to look at either the lights or Jonathan.

"Or how about the greens?"

"I don't know."

"I like the oranges myself. Do you like them?"

Patiently: "I don't know."

From beneath the tree Jonathan was able to hear amazing things. He wasn't out of sight; but in the same way young children believe they are hiding themselves by covering their eyes, Jodi's family seemed to think that words said to someone other than Jonathan could not be heard by him. "We should make things up to scare Jonathan," giggled Kristin to Phil, one of her brothers-in-law. She put her hand on his arm to indicate her proposal shouldn't be taken seriously. "By saying the game was canceled by bad weather before it could be finished, for example. That would nullify everything, wouldn't it?"

"I think it would. But weather never cancels football games."

"Or we could say" – here the giggle was louder and the touch more significant – "the sheriff heard there was illegal gambling in town." Kristin began to lose control of her laughter. She used her hand to cover her mouth. "Tim hangs around with some of those deputies, I bet. He could have one of them come over and make a fake arrest."

Jonathan straightened up and looked around for Jodi. They hadn't discussed when to begin the return trip, but now that dinner was over and the early winter nightfall approaching, preparing to leave might be the thing to do. Anticipation of leaving brought out a bit of wildness in Jonathan. "Have you been tested for color blindness?" he asked.

"I don't know."

The first thing Jonathan saw as he searched for Jodi was looming hair. "So," said Hillary, approaching with an interested smile set two or more feet below her apex. "What are we going to do with all those winnings?" She winked.

Jonathan gave another, somewhat more frantic, look around the room and lifted himself on his toes to see into the next. "Jodi and I really haven't had much time to discuss it."

"Jodi? Are you in so deep that you need her permission?"

"He'll do what every good gambler does," said Phil, who had overheard. "Roll the money into the next bet."

Jonathan wondered if this was intended to be malicious. Phil didn't look malicious. "First thing first. I haven't even collected the money yet."

"How you go about collecting – that's a story worth hearing, I'd bet." Hillary moved closer for an instant, apparently in a mock attempt to bump one of her hips against one of Jonathan's hips. Though she looked somewhat troubled by the thuggish aspects of what she imagined to be involved in collecting gambling debts.

"A guy at work runs the pool. He'll pay out tomorrow. Have you seen Jodi?"

Hillary put an arm around Jonathan's shoulders. Her hair creaked under the strain of its weight. "I'm glad you're going to be part of the family."

"Am I the last to know again?" said Phil.

"Well, you *are*, Jonathan, whether you two have announced it or not. Maybe you haven't even admitted it to each other. But you *know* you are."

There was no way to escape this conversation, Jonathan thought, but to be conspiratorial. He gave Hillary his best look of joint venture, a look intended to acknowledge the clueless speculation the rest of the world must be engaged in about *them*, Jonathan and Hillary – he gave his look, Hillary returned the tight smile and significant eyes, and in a burst of nausea Jonathan was gone. He threaded his way through spools of potential relatives, all the *J*s and *K*s and nephews and nieces, veering to avoid a Bob here, stepping aside for a Bobby there. The rec room had emptied: West Virginia and Tennessee were done. Overheard condolences told Jonathan that Tim's twenty dollars had been lost. Jonathan stepped into the kitchen and there, against the far wall with her mother, stood Jodi. She was troubled.

Instinct told Jonathan not to enter this conversation. He observed a full minute from across the small kitchen, which was a safe enough distance; Jodi and her mother were too preoccupied to notice anyone beyond the other. She, Jodi, was pleading. Making some sort of case, trying to be persuasive, carrying the conversation, but all from a position of weakness displayed in obvious entreaty. For her part Mrs. Amundson listened sympathetically, but responded to her daughter's appeals with implacable certainty. She did this with only the slightest shake of her head, a simultaneous expression of kindness and intransigence. As though it were a decade earlier and the day of Jodi's first school dance.

Jodi spied Jonathan and immediately brought the conversation with her mother to a close. She stepped toward him. "Do you have a moment?" she asked.

"Me?"

"Daddy wants to see you."

"Okay." Baffled, he followed Jodi into an entryway that was in essence a shed tacked on to the back of the house. Benches lined both sides, largely unusable due to the coats and overalls overhanging from wall hooks. Boots scattered out of their pairs obstructed the way to a door leading out to the yard and, eventually, to the barn. Jodi plucked a wool jacket for Jonathan and another for herself. She led him into the cold dry air. "Whose do you think this is?" Jonathan asked as he wrestled with his jacket. The difficulty was a feed cap stuffed into one of the sleeves. "Tim's or your father's?"

"I can't say what this is all about," Jodi said in a voice that made Jonathan suspect she could. She was unhappy. Jonathan worked hard to keep up with her as she followed the shoveled path the sixty yards from the back of the farmhouse to the barn. "My advice would be to do more listening than talking." She was huffing with vigor.

"I can do that."

"Daddy," Jodi called. A door to the barn was open and Jodi peered into the blackness. It was a depthless black, contrasting sharply with the blinding white of the snow and the sky overhead, patches of blue and colorlessness quilted together.

"It's Jonathan I want to talk to."

Jodi glanced at Jonathan and bit her lip anxiously. "I'm here," he said, stepping into the doorway.

"You can go back in, Jodi," Mr. Amundson said. "No use getting chilled on Christmas." Jodi retreated, unsure whether her father could see her, but did not turn toward the house. Instead she stepped to the side, into calf-deep snow, and moved close to the far side of the doorway. Jonathan ventured further into the barn. His eyes began to adjust to the cool gloom and suddenly he saw the figure of Jodi's father. He was close enough to cause Jonathan a reflexive and mirthless laugh.

"Jonathan," Mr. Amundson said. "Do you really want me to call you Jonathan?" It was a complicated voice: relaxed but purposeful and, to Jonathan's ear, flavored with menace.

"Everyone else does. It's my name." Meant to be said with good cheer, artificially flippant. He and Jodi's father stood nearer than Jonathan would have preferred, had he a choice. They were fifteen or more feet in from the doorway; Jodi, out of sight, remained outside, as her father may or may not have been aware.

"You're in control, aren't you, Jonathan."

"Pardon?"

"Life doesn't have you. You have life." This was a Bill Amundson different from the baffled figurehead inside the house; something had been stirred, Jonathan grasped, by Tim's outburst.

"By the tail, do you mean? In that sense?"

"Money comes easy to you. Not always from work and reward."

Was that what this was all about? "The office pool," Jonathan said with a chuckle meant to convey deprecation.

"The thing about it is that you've found a way to make that kind of money through something besides a paycheck. It's like found money."

"Or the payoff on a wise investment."

Jodi's father cleared his throat. Something in the far dark made a sound, then something else: a cow breath, maybe, followed by a shudder from another large beast. Then a quick flutter and a hop or two upon what sounded to be straw. This was a real barn, Jonathan noted, a subplot to the lecture from Jodi's father. Men and animals standing in the dark together, under the same roof. Jonathan tried to appreciate the silliness of it.

"It's not worth keeping, Jonathan. You'd be better off without it. It'd be wrong to keep it. And it's needed."

Needed by the church, Jonathan guessed. So he was about to be asked to make a thirty-five hundred dollar donation. Itself an investment, a bulk purchase of family approval, and therefore probably not objectionable. Probably wise. Not that his and Jodi's blueprints would necessarily be those upon which her brothers and sisters had relied.

"What would you like me to do?"

Mr. Amundson's voice became friendlier. "Use it to help Tim. He's buying into the farm – it's been a plan for quite a while now. Jodi's mother and I are willing to turn it over to him over time, and for a reasonable price. But he's needed some help jump-starting the payments. That's where you could help."

"I think I have mixed feelings about that," said Jonathan. This was a portion of what he thought.

"About the money going to Tim? In that sense?" Was this mimicry? The thought of it – the horror of even the possibility of being mocked by a probable father-in-law – left Jonathan temporarily speechless. Well, yes. In that sense. It was found money, nice to have won but dispensable. But to hand it over to Tim so he could hand it over to Jodi's father . . . . Maybe this was more a test of intelligence than commitment.

But before Jonathan could articulate his tumult of responses a cry came from the open door. "Uh uh!" screeched Jodi. She was silhouetted against the rectangle of snow glare behind her, knees high as she navigated the drift that had formed at the doorway. "That's out of the question." The decisiveness caught Jonathan by surprise – it was aimed at her father, after all, and made even more scandalous by it being Christmas Day.

"This is our conversation," Mr. Amundson said. "Me and Jonathan."

"Come on." She had Jonathan's arm. There was heat in

her voice. Jodi led Jonathan out into the yard but not toward the house. Instead she angled around it, toward the front. Toward the long driveway and the Mesa Climber.

"I'm in someone else's coat," Jonathan objected. This was shorthand for the mess being created: wrong clothes taken, wrong clothes left, not to mention unopened gifts for and from Jodi's family, certainly not to mention a rift that was likely to define him and Jodi with her family for a generation or two. And yet there was a thrill to this. What a declaration of independence. What a story to tell.

"Oh God," Jodi said. She stopped abruptly and gave Jonathan a look of consternation. It had occurred to her, he grasped, that the keys were likely in a pocket of Jonathan's new coat, still hanging inside the house. They needed to cross back over the bridge they had just set aflame. Or they were the bandits realizing their getaway car had been towed from the handicapped zone in front of the bank. But Jonathan felt the keys against his leg. "These?" He pulled out the key ring and the two of them rapidly ascended the Mesa Climber. As they did, Jonathan was seized with a new and greater sense of doom. Jodi recognized the horror. Behind the Mesa Climber was John and Stacy's minivan, then John and Staci's, followed by Carol's pickup, an unidentified Saturn, a teenager car, colored metal all the long way to the county road, a hundred and a half feet of interference.

"God!" said Jodi. Then, for emphasis: "Shit!"

A crowd had gathered at the window. Views of Jodi and Jonathan sitting behind the windshield had democratically been distributed to each *J* and *K* and every interested grandchild, at least a dozen faces in all, even two small eyes, it seemed, peering from the interior of Hillary's column of hair, making Hillary and her nephew appear to be members of the same blonde totem pole. Jonathan, watching the faces through two panes of glass and, sandwiched between them, twenty yards of winter air, was unable to determine how the crowd was taking this. Was he seeing smiles? Or simple curiosity? They were good people, he thought magnanimously, to the extent he knew enough to offer a judgment. They would remember all this a long time, speak of it often. Someday, years from now, they would tease Jonathan about it. Jonathan pushed the foreboding from his mind. The immediate problem was inertia. He and Jodi in the front seat, a substantial part of the family massed around the picture window, he and Jodi king and queen, perhaps, but the others knights and rooks and bishops and strategically-placed pawns, everyone wondering whose turn was next. Something had to give.

Tim gave. It was unclear from where he emerged; Jonathan simply heard a noise at his elbow and turned with a start to see Tim's scowl and hear the metallic punch of the driver's door as it swung open. "Move," Tim commanded with authority, and to get out of the way Jonathan slid between the seats and to his knees in the back. Tim pulled himself up into the leather and took hold of the steering wheel, turning the key in the same motion.

"Tim," his sister said, but it wasn't an objection. It was curiosity, Jonathan decided, perhaps even gratitude.

"Lover Boy sure wasn't going to do anything." Then, almost as an afterthought: "You two look stupid." Tim glanced back, past Jonathan, and with a turn of the wheel and an explosion of gasoline vapor the Mesa Climber backed off the driveway and onto the frozen and snow-crusted lawn, curling wide to avoid the minivan behind. Jonathan was glad to be only a spectator to this recklessness, though thrill was involved also. Tim expertly guided the three of them, at a high rate of speed, around a yard light, through the corner of a sprawl of dormant shrubbery, and over a string of brightly crunching Christmas lights the night wind had carried down from an adjacent pine. The journey was stop-and-start as the tires spun on snow crystals and then grabbed a vulnerable patch of lawn, pitching muddy clods high into the air. The Mesa Climber dipped into the ditch separating the yard from the road, plowed beneath the brittle ice while sloshing brown water to the side, then, after a moment of uncertainty, charged up the far bank and arrived triumphantly on the county road, diagonally.

"Bravo!" Jodi cheered. Indeed; except that this stunt, memorialized in the looping parallel lines visible beside the long and entire length of driveway, demanded an explanation. Jonathan felt sure of it.

Tim brushed aside his sister's admiration and turned back toward Jonathan. "She's all yours," he said. Then, continuing to address Jonathan but shifting his gaze toward his sister: "Plug her all you want."

"Tim!" Jodi said angrily.

"And" – looking at Jonathan again – "keep on betting on that grid."

"Not to give the money to you I won't," Jonathan said crisply.

"Damn right. Don't ever give in to the old man."

Jodi's indignation softened into perplexity. "You know that Daddy asked for the money."

"Of course I know that Daddy asked for the money. It was the first thing I thought of when Lover Boy started lording that big number over all us poor sodbusters."

"All of you are so unfair," Jodi said bitterly.

"It's not the money," Jonathan said. "Who gives a damn about the money?"

Tim narrowed his eyes at this demonstration of wealth so abundant it allowed for the casual abandonment of three and a half thousand dollars. "I don't want help in paying my father. I want to *fail* at paying my father." He said this while opening the long door of the Mesa Climber and stepping down onto the hard road.

Jonathan remained in the back seat, uncertain as to what should happen next. Jodi looked at her feet, too upset with this turn of events to do anything but will herself down the highway; she was, Jonathan was sure, thinking of the apartment and December 26. Far across the yard, too far really to be seen in detail, Jodi's family watched without discernible expression.

"Now get back up in this seat," Tim said with a commanding and disdainful patience, "and put this thing into gear. And then drive down that road" – he pointed toward the horizon, turning his shoulders away from the farm – "and don't come back." He smiled a smile that began as manipulation but broke in spite of itself into guileless joy at the recreation of this sustained attack, even as he knew it would soon be over and the prevailing order would reassert itself. "Not ever."

Melodrama, Jonathan thought. He had no appetite for challenging Tim and certainly none for salvaging something of the day. To his side he caught Jodi's fierce attempt to hold back tears. Without a word Jonathan did exactly as Tim had suggested. He moved to the driver's seat and began to ease the Mesa Climber down the road. The rear view mirror presented Tim as diminishing, one foot on the roadway's black asphalt and one on the shoulder sloping toward his father's farmhouse. Looking, Jonathan imagined, engaging in his own melodrama, like a soldier after the battle, or a father after the wedding, or the last tree on the cleared horizon, or a penned animal exercising its calibrated freedoms.

Losing Camille

A couple of months ago, right in the middle of everything (Fourth of July weekend?), Cammy showed me this photograph Cade had given her. It was their second grade class picture, thirty kids taking up about as much space as a picnic blanket, the girls sad-faced in their ribbons and hair bands and the boys with clueless smiles and all their little nubby parts. And there, in the very front row, is Cammy standing next to Cade. We just howled at the randomness. "It was fate!" I said to Cammy. A couple of months ago – not so long, really – I wanted Cammy to tell me everything about Cade, but to get anywhere I had to use my brain. You don't tease Cammy too much. You don't act like you're at a slumber party.

That picture means she and Cade knew each other ten years before deciding to pair up. Amazing. I remember when it first dawned on me that something was happening between Cammy and Cade. So strange, it really was, that this should happen to our quiet, content Camille. Cade was a big jock, basketball player and all – the type most girls in school might flip over (but not Cammy) if they thought they had a chance. I don't know what he did. He couldn't have just asked her for a date out of the blue; Cammy would've said no. He couldn't have thrown out some creepy line like so many guys do – "Wanna take a ride in the backseat of my car," crap like that – because it never would've worked with Cammy. But he did something. Did it happen graduation night? From my chair (front and center, me being Ninth Grade Delegate to Student Council) I watched and Cade, sitting on stage next to Cammy, leaned over during the address and whispered something and Cammy smiled. Then the next weekend, during Cammy's party, he stopped at the house. Well, everyone came to that party, half the senior class and all the teachers, but Cade came alone, not with his usual buddies, the letter jacket crowd. (Lyndie was standing next to me when he came in, and she leaned on me as if in a swoon and said, just loud enough for me only to hear, "Cade Livingston! Cade Livingston!" over and over until I had to give her a little shove and a stare. Ladies and gentlemen: Lyndie.) He stayed about a half hour, and I don't even think he said more than hi to Cammy. But a few days later he came running by the front yard, Captain Marathon, and Mom and Cammy and I happened to be getting out of the car from some place and Cade yelled – no, not "Hi, Cammy!" since that doesn't work with her – he yelled, "Hi, Rachel!" And Cammy giggled! That was the whole key, that giggle should have tipped me off; but I was confused that he even knew my name, and was trying to fend off Mom's look, and thinking of Lyndie, half relieved she wasn't there and half wishing she was.

And then one night, maybe two weeks later, Cade was over for supper. Mom found out five minutes to six and went into a fit since we were having chicken salad sandwiches. Cammy was wearing that white button-down sweater of hers, the one she keeps in the front closet, and when Cade knocked she walked to the door slowly, looking cute, I thought: tall, thin Cammy, with that long straight hair and perfect face. Dad's so funny, he noticed nothing until he sat down and looked up and spotted Cade across the table, and tried to act cool by saying hi, casually, except that he mixed Cade up with Joey Swanson, who was also on the basketball team, and said, "Hi, Joey." And the table just exploded, me and Mom and Cammy and Cade too. When everything settled down I watched Cammy and she looked at Cade, a two-of-us/three-of-them look, and then she looked down at her plate, unable to get the smile off her face. Only then did my nimble brain understand that something had happened. Cammy had fallen into love.

After that we never saw her. Cammy spent the summer working in a women's shop at the mall, and when she got home about four o'clock she would change clothes and be gone. She and Cade would go to the mall, or a movie or ballgame, or to Cade's folks', or down to the college, where Cade was going to play basketball that next year – I guess they went about everywhere. One night Cammy came in about twelve-thirty, I had just turned off the light. The house was absolutely still, and I could hear her switch on the light in her room (our bedrooms sharing a wall as they do), and then the rustle of her clothes as she undressed, and the whole time she was humming something softly to herself. It was "Summer, Summer, Summer," the catchy version that was always on the radio then. Followed by the light being switched off and the bounce of her mattress and then she was in bed, maybe three minutes in all since coming in the front door. I'd wake up at nine or so and she'd already be gone for work.

Mom and Dad were in some kind of terror about all this. Not that they said anything, not at first. But their faces had this dumb look of apprehension, like goldfish watching someone introduce a new fish, the wrong kind, into their bowl. I don't blame them, everything was just happening out of nowhere, I sure didn't know what to make of it either. If it had been me they maybe wouldn't have cared (though obviously *I* couldn't have come jingling in at twelve-thirty, four nights in a row), but they had plans for Cammy, and *Cammy* had plans for Cammy. She was going to Oberlin, had wanted to go since eighth grade, and she not only got admitted, she got the scholarship. She was to leave end of August. But now she was losing her head over a local kid – that's what Mom and Dad thought, I'm sure of it – and throwing everything into jeopardy. I mean, it was like eighteen years were spent pursuing this goal and then two months away she suddenly loses interest. And Mom and Dad would see Cade over some evening – tall and good-looking and sweet, treating Cammy real nice – and then they would see Cammy as though she had been brainwashed, changed from content and serious to beaming with happiness – they must have thought it was hopeless, that they had lost her and she had lost herself.

But I've never seen anyone so happy. I don't mean Cammy was cartwheeling through the house or suddenly loud or anything. She was still reserved, dignified in that Cammy sort of way. But she had changed. In a lot of ways the new Cammy was even better than the old, but all the same the old Cammy was gone, and I missed her. When I told that to Sarah (who has her head on tighter than Lyndie), told her I just sort of felt left behind, she said she'd seen Cammy and Cade around town and they were *always* laughing, she said. Well, that's it, isn't it? That's the thought you fall asleep with: they make each other happier than they'd been before they started going out.

About the third week or so in July Cade went off for ten days of basketball camp. I think Cammy got four letters – *letters* – in those ten days Cade was gone. Four letters from a *guy*, and you know how likely a guy is to ever write, especially when marooned in a gym where they spend half the time bouncing balls and the other half studying about bouncing balls. I have no idea how many letters Cammy sent. But when she got home from work a letter would usually be there, and before anything else she'd take it up to her room, wouldn't even open the envelope before closing her bedroom door. Then she would come down a little more talkative than before, happy but composed, her mind off somewhere else.

Cade's first night back, Cammy spent a lot of time getting ready, put on her best dress, worked on the hair. Mom was scared to death, I'm sure, thinking Cammy'd be getting engaged that night or something. "Big night!" I teased Cammy. "Don't forget the glass slippers!" She only smiled. "If you're thinking royal ball, that's next month." And she told me about some big dance evening in August at the pavilion out on Genevieve Lake, she and Cade had tickets that had cost forty dollars apiece or something, including dinner, and there would be an orchestra, and as she was talking the doorbell rang and there was our basketball star. He was in a jacket, tie hanging down the front for all to see, and I got that little thrill you feel when you see someone different than you're used to seeing them. Everything in the house just sort of stopped a second; I mean, he was gorgeous. Even Mom did a little double look and saw that I saw her do it and then she went to check on the leftovers she'd been warming up for me and Dad. A second after Mom went into the kitchen Cammy walked up to Cade and hugged him and gave him a little short kiss, probably not wanting Mom to see but not caring, I guess, that I was right there.

I was up when Cammy got home, it was only about eleven or so, and I went into her room. She was sitting on her bed, taking off earrings.

"Where did you go?" I said.

"Down to Elk River. Have you ever heard of Bangkok Temple?"

I shook my head.

"Thai, of course. Wonderful."

"You had a great time," I said.

Cammy gave me this funny look, maybe because she was having trouble with her earring. "Yeah, but I think ten days of bouncing basketballs can have its effect."

"Cammy," I giggled, proud that she would tell me that. As though we girls were in the know, joining the ages of women in perpetual amusement over their boys' peculiarities.

"It was strange, that's all. Some nights are like that."

At first it seemed like everything was like before. The next day Cammy went to work and when she got home she called and then biked over to Cade's house. And then returned between eight and nine, right as it was starting to get dark. The rest of us were working on a jigsaw puzzle of Old Faithful.

"This is a pleasant surprise," Mom said. "Cade didn't go back to basketball camp, did he?" Which sounds cruel, but Mom didn't intend it that way – how could she? She couldn't dislike Cade, even if she didn't like what she thought was happening to Cammy. Cammy stopped and watched us a minute or two, helped find a couple of pieces, then went upstairs. "It's not the same Camille," Mom said. "She's so wrapped up in Cade that she doesn't think anything or anyone else exists."

The next day Sarah and Lyndie and I went to the lake. It was near the first of August, one of those beautiful summer days when the sun rises miles and miles and then stops in the sky, and we stayed the entire afternoon. When I got home, around five o'clock, Cammy was on her phone and quiet. "Okay," she said, then was quiet about thirty seconds, then said "okay" again, in an agitated sort of way, then was quiet for awhile before saying "okay" again, so softly I could barely hear. She started to put the phone away and I went fast out the back door so Cammy wouldn't know I had overheard. Mom was in the garden. "You just get home?" she said when she saw me.

"Just now."

"Is Camille still here?" she said.

"Still here."

"That's a wonder," Mom said, and it made me disgusted, so I just put my towel on the clothesline and went inside. See, Mom saw the same thing day after day: Cammy getting home from work, calling Cade, leaving and not coming home until late after we had all gone to bed. So it's natural, maybe, she felt like she did, but I was starting to see something was wrong. Cammy was watching TV, looking tired and in a bad mood, and neither of us said anything. "How was swimming?" Cammy finally asked, but she didn't seem interested in my answer. Swimming had been great, actually, the days then being so hot and muggy and still. We watched TV some more, no conversation, and I thought about that night when Cade had come for supper, how Cammy had been wearing that sweater, and with the current heat that seemed like a long, long time ago, and for the first time all summer I thought about the new school year coming and that it was time to get up and going again.

Supper was tense, Cammy and Mom being quarrelsome, me caught in the middle and Dad mostly oblivious. Mom kept trying to get Dad involved, but he didn't understand, or wouldn't understand, what was happening. After Cammy left the table, but while I was still there, Dad really got the looks. Not dirty looks, more like "can't you see I need help" looks. Then I left and Mom and Dad stayed at the table for a long time afterwards.

Cammy was like she was caged, going from her bedroom to the TV and then out to the yard and back in again, not wanting to be alone but not wanting to talk to anyone either. Finally, about dark, we were all four watching TV, things seemed to have calmed down, and right after Mom got up to get something Cammy got up too, and said she was going out. We heard her get in the car and start it up, back out the driveway, then Mom came back and just stared at the room, like a guy looking in his wallet and seeing a lot less money than he thought should have been there. "Camille wanted to take the car," Dad said. "Uh huh," Mom said.

Cammy was gone a long time. It started to become obvious that something was going to happen that night, that Mom and Dad had no intention of going to bed until Cammy got home. Finally I went upstairs, eleven o'clock or so, and read some magazines for about an hour. Then I shut off the light and laid on top of the bed, eyes open. The house was absolutely still. Another twenty minutes or so went by and I heard the car come up the driveway, and then Cammy came in the house and straight upstairs and into her room. There was some stirring downstairs and pretty soon I can hear Dad's steps in the hallway. There's a knock on Cammy's door and he goes in and starts some small talk, Cammy not saying anything. Then Dad said what he came up to say.

I made out most of what Dad said, and what I couldn't really hear I could imagine. You know: "You're experiencing something new in your life," and "Love's a wonderful thing, but a powerful thing, too," and "No one knows how strong their emotions can be, or how they'll react to them," and "I'm telling you this because your mother and I care about you and your future." Yes, I had to lie there and hear it right along with Cammy, the same speech I'll hear directly someday, no doubt. I tried to turn my head and close my eyes, honestly, but who's kidding who, I was wide awake and fascinated and thinking that a terrible thing was happening, the biggest of mistakes. Finally Dad left and walked downstairs and I heard the folks' bedroom door creak shut and then everything was quiet, except for Cammy breathing in a jerky sort of way, just loud enough for me to hear, a strange sound until I realized it was the sound of her crying.

Cammy was sick the next day and missed work, and when she came down for supper it was a different Cammy, the third of the summer. She had been defeated. I was thinking it was the next few days that would be hard for Cammy, but those days passed and, though I began expecting her to come back to life, nothing changed. The whole house got dragged down pretty soon, all of us surly and tired of each other and just plain hurt. How that can happen I don't know, a good, happy family torn apart, but it was happening. Mom and Dad knew it, figured out why what was happening was happening, understanding finally that things between Cammy and Cade had blown apart, and Mom and Dad tried to get us back to what we used to be. It was Dad's idea, random, cheesy even, that we all go out one evening to eat ice cream sundaes, sitting at a picnic table back from the beach like we used to; but it worked in a way, it was a real fun night, Cammy and Mom giggling with each other and me and Dad just happy to have everyone at peace. Cammy and Mom went for a walk when we got home, coming back with red eyes and arms around each other.

But the next morning came and at breakfast I saw in Cammy's face that ice cream sundaes can only do so much. Oh, August was an awful month. Awful.

Cammy spent a lot of time to herself. She was always a loner, but now she was practically a hermit, sitting in her room hour after hour, just – well, I didn't know *what* she was doing until late one night when she just decided to go walk. Out the front door she went, leaving her bedroom door half open, the light on, and on her bed was an open notebook with a pen on top. One part of me hates myself for walking over to her bed and looking, but I let myself think it was the most important thing in the world for me to know what was going on with Cammy. It was a journal, of course. I read it quickly, about five pages in two minutes or so, and it was Cammy all right, the *real* Cammy, the Cammy we know is there but don't hear from often. It was all about Cade, little bits about what he had said, and when, or promised, plans they had made, like the Genevieve Lake Dance that had now come and gone and been missed, and Cammy seemed to be building up some case to convince herself that what had happened *couldn't* have happened. Part of it was smart Cammy, asking things like "I wonder if for me Cade represented high school and home and Peavey, and I wanted to hold on to him as a way of holding on to those things." Then she wrote like it was maybe the opposite, she saw in him some possibilities she'd never seen before, he was a door to a new world or something. And Cammy went on like that, wondering, not really accomplishing anything. Finally at the end she said, the last thing she wrote before leaving the room, "It's no use hoping that it's not over, because it really is, and the sooner I understand that, the better off I'll be. I've got to remember that I was able to be happy before I ever noticed Cade." *Cammy* said that, my big sister. I want to say I felt so sorry for Cammy, and I did, but more than that I just felt frightened. I walked back to my room and looked at my bed and all those big stuffed animals my friends laugh at. Teddy bears for teenagers, Sarah says, but that night I was glad they were there.

One night, right near the end of the summer, Lyndie and Sarah and I were at the DQ, the only place to hang out in a town like Peavey, and who should be across the parking lot but a bunch of older guys, including Cade. They were eating ice cream and kicking around a can, two had gloves and were playing catch. Just waiting for the summer to end, like us. My friends saw them but didn't mention it, knowing about Cade and Cammy. Pretty soon I look up and see Cade coming across the lot to us and I want to start walking, but instead I wait and wonder what to think. I hated Cade because Cammy did, probably, and I thought a lot of him because I knew him, but the thing he had done – well, all those thoughts jumbled in my head and I had absolutely no idea what he was up to. Sarah sort of rounded Lyndie over to see some kids we knew, so no one was there but Cade and me. And Cade said, nice and respectful, kind of tentative, "How are you doing, Rachel?"

"Good," I said, just hoping to say the things Cammy would want me to say.

"How's everything at home?" he said, to which I said, "Fine." Then he said, "Your Dad doing fine?" with a smile, no doubt thinking of how Dad called him Joey Swanson, and it hit me that there were family secrets that weren't just ours anymore. "He's okay," I said.

"And Cammy?"

"Okay."

"Well, good," Cade said, and I guess I thought he'd ask me what she was doing or how she was spending her time, that he'd be at least curious, but he didn't ask, just shifted like *he* was the one uncomfortable, and said, "Your sister's quite a woman," saying *woman* instead of *girl* to show how mature he was, I guess, and understanding of things beyond my comprehension. What do I say to this? I wondered, and wished Sarah was back with me, who would have known.

"You've got school soon," Cade said, and I just sort of nodded, looking over for my friends. "What, a couple of weeks?" he said. "Something like that," I said.

Cade looked toward some car passing on the road, then to me, and said, "Just thought I'd stop over and say hi," and as he began walking back I said, without having thought about it – thinking would have *kept* me from saying it – I said, "Who's your new Cammy?"

He turned around as though amazed I could talk. "No one else," he said, real surprised. "I mean, of course not." I kept my eyes on him and he went on, saying, "It's just something with me. I like your sister a lot, but not like she likes me. Not anymore. I don't know why. I know I hurt Cammy a lot." He said it all in a pained sort of way, rushing some words and leaving big gaps between others, and later when I told Sarah she said, sarcastically, oh of course, if it's something he really can't understand then he can't be responsible for it, right? So it's not his fault, it just happened, and here he is out with the guys and tell me: where's Cammy? Cammy was home, of course, and I knew exactly what Sarah was saying, but she didn't hear Cade and if she had she might have felt the way I did. It was a bad feeling, knowing that someone could do to another what Cade had done to Cammy; but to know it wasn't really Cade who had done anything was worse. I knew Cammy hurt bad and so *someone* was to blame; but blaming Cade didn't seem right, either. It all confuses me. I thought about it a lot that night, until I didn't want to think about it anymore.

Cammy's last night came soon after that. She was up late: packing and rearranging and cleaning seemed to be an endless job. I stayed in my room, reading magazines until almost midnight, when I knocked on Cammy's door and went in. "This room's never been this clean," I said, like Mom would, and though it *was* clean, the thing that jumped out at you was the emptiness.

"It never has," Cammy agreed, looking around. "I've got almost everything in the hallway downstairs. Hope it all fits in the car." She sat on the bed and let out a big sigh, and I could see she was exhausted. It was so sad, really, to think about her leaving and wondering if she'd ever be anything but a guest here again. All the mornings we used to get ready for school, and eating suppers together at night, then watching stupid TV, one day after another, seeming so routine, so *unimportant*, and now Cammy was moving out. But Cammy was real good about it, trying to make me feel good, and we talked, sister to sister, a half hour or so. She had her radio on, real low, and there was some end-of-summer wrap-up on, "Summer, Summer, Summer" and all the other songs that had been popular.

"This is good timing for me," Cammy said. "It's time for me to go to college." Well, she didn't really have a choice, did she? I mean, it seemed like saying, on your birthday, "This is a good day to have a birthday." Good or bad, a birthday's a birthday and there's not much say you have about it. I didn't tell that to Cammy, of course. "It's time for something different," she said.

We talked mostly about me, Mom and Dad, little things. Just to distract ourselves. I went to bed feeling empty and just wishing she'd be gone and everything would be back to as close to normal as it could be.

Everything did in fact fit into the car, though it was close, and we rode with all this cargo down to Minneapolis. The bus driver there shook his head but ended up packing everything underneath for us. Then we said goodbye, it was awful for everyone, and Cammy left, real brave I thought, and we drove home, me wishing my own school had started so that I'd have some homework to do. Summer's great, the way we slip away from the requirements, but those harnesses are there for a reason and it's possible, I'd seen, for all that freedom to turn against you.

That was two weeks ago. I stayed out of the house a lot the first few days, then school *did* start for me, happily. The night before high school began Mom went into Cammy's room, why I don't know. She just stood there at the door looking, then walked over to the bed to straighten the bedspread, which of course didn't need straightening since the bed hadn't been slept in. Parents get real used to eighteen years of a daughter, I'm sure. After a minute or so Mom left, sniffling, her eyes a little wet, even; I was in the hall and saw her. But Cammy *wanted* to go away to Ohio, I thought, and Mom wanted her to go, too – got real upset when she thought Cammy might *not* go. Things that seem so simple are pretty complicated sometimes, and you can spend a lot of time trying to straighten it all out without getting anywhere. I just went back into my room rather than say anything, since the only thing I could think to say was that there sure has been a lot of crying in this house lately.

So now the school year's begun, I'm a sophomore, and this whole world has created itself again, crowded halls and bells, Student Council posters, endless chatter. It's different not having Cammy's class around, not her or her friends or the guys. It's a new atmosphere. I walk to school since it's still warm, sometimes with Lyndie but mostly alone. By the time I get there a bunch of guys are always playing basketball on the outside courts, yelling and shooting and showing off. Cute guys, too, and they know things are dawning for them, pretty soon they'll be the varsity players, the Cade Livingstons of our class. Sometimes I stop and watch them, knowing full well that most girls won't because the guys want them to. So what? Then I head on in to make the bell, get to first hour English, smile at Lyndie as she makes eyes at our new teacher; but what I'm really thinking about is that the day can't come soon enough when I'll be able to get up and out of this town.

Rule of 100

Plans

Of course the fever caught up with her
the day of the senior prom, marked signal red

on her calendar these last three months.
How could it have not, what with the exhaustion

of the dress, the hair, cremes and appointments,
instant messages buzzing like bees from flower to flower?

So now she lies on the basement couch, deep inside
her bathrobe as any egg in its nest, warmed

by her mother's tea, and the clock strikes ten.
To the drum of rain she pages through the big books

from childhood – elegant princesses in fairy tales,
salmon colored castles and blue horses –

attuned to remembered detail and, though she can't
admit it, not yet, happy.

The poem arrived in an envelope bearing no return address. It was neatly typed and there was no identification on the page. Joe Czelarc, who knew nothing of poetry – who, not to put too fine a point on it, disdained, even feared, poetry – nevertheless knew enough to know this was no schoolboy exercise. There was something to the poem, a sophistication. The way it talked about a prom and then said the girls' instant messages buzzed *like bees from flower to flower*. And then there was *the big books from childhood*; Czelarc liked that. He threw away the envelope but saved the poem in a desk drawer.

Czelarc's college had required an English class for graduation, and there had been a poetry unit. The class had been useless; worse, it had provided a way for those inclined toward such things to segregate themselves from those, like Czelarc, who were not. An affinity for poetry was a predictor of so many other traits, Czelarc had observed, traits that should have had nothing to do with stringing words in lines. You'd see them trekking to and from the neighborhood co-op, these poetry admirers. Petitioning for this or that – getting the vending machines removed from campus, for instance. They would distribute their election fliers. But the worst was this attitude, this *certainty*, that the things people like Czelarc cared about had little to do with how a life should actually be lived. They had smiles for the misconception.

They were fooling themselves. Czelarc's successes hadn't surprised him at all. The right combination of characteristics – he was self-assured and worked hard; he was tall and had a large face, attractive without being threatening – made older men, men with wealth, comfortable with Czelarc. They had given him a little money at first, curious as to what he might do with it. Czelarc acquired a real estate license, bought and repaired a handful of duplexes. He obtained a mortgage license and partnered with a contractor he had known from high school. On a leap of faith the two built a small strip mall that snagged a national tenant and made Czelarc's reputation. After that the trust and the money came easily. If you had a lot of money there was a little portion you wanted to be sure to invest with Joe Czelarc. On Czelarc's fortieth birthday he opened Phoenix, an entire community of houses built on what had previously been cornfield. All of Phoenix's houses were large; Czelarc's was the largest.

Phoenix seemed the right name, Czelarc thought, because that was his story: rising from the ashes. He had been an only child, when you got right down to it – Mark had left for the navy when Joe was still an infant. Czelarc's parents had divorced the year Joe entered kindergarten. His mother moved out to California to be near a sister and had been dead twenty years now. Czelarc's father, a gasoline man, ran a profitable station but could be aloof, cranky, fatalistic. Bitter, sometimes. At closing one night he had sighed and said to Joe (in high school then, and being taught the ropes), "I know how a kid like you thinks. When I was your age I did the same, regarding life the way a boy regards a pond, assuming the fish."

Two other things Czelarc heard from his father – who was a silent man, generally, though given to occasional speeches – remained especially strong in memory. One had to do with the way money was made, the way a city pushes itself forward. "People always complain about old buildings coming down," Czelarc's father had said, "and how fast this town is changing. But it's the opposite that's true. It's the town that's built to last. You only have to look at the old pictures to know that. People, they're the ones who bloom and wither" – *bloom and wither*: Joe remembered that, the phrase being so unlike the way his father talked – "and move up and out, heading for the hills." That had been an old joke: the city cemeteries were clustered on the town's highest hill. "Up and down the streets," his father had continued, "learning what's what. Then they push on. How much of a thought do you think they ever give that they're only in some earlier's shoes? Or that the hospital is full of babies waiting to take their place?" His father's words, spoken a quarter of a century ago, most often resurfaced during zoning meetings, as Czelarc endured somebody's speech – everyone had his speech – about preserving some abandoned storefront from development.

And there was this: "I've worked hard," his father had said, "to avoid life." By which he meant that life was an obstacle course, the purpose of it all being to avoid the bad marriage, the accident, financial ruin, illness. Czelarc's father believed he had done this, more or less – the obstacles had only bruised him, at any rate, and he had clambered past each one. But having children had meant running the risks all over again, vicariously. "It's like swimming damn shark waters," Joe remembered hearing, usually late in the evening. "You make one shore and then dive right back in to head back to the other."

Czelarc made use of his father's words. At dinner, using a laugh apparently free of bitterness, he would tell the men who financed him that having Joe Czelarc as a son ranked right up there with swimming shark-infested waters. He often told the story while discussing Phoenix; the contrast, his father's expectations and then the reality, was irresistible. "When you chose that name you chose well," Alan Wheatley had once said. "I like the classical allusion." Czelarc hadn't known how to reply.

Within a month of Wheatley's remark Czelarc found himself at a large commercial closing. He had brokered the sale of a warehouse in the industrial park, cementing the agreement by persuading the parties to submit to a creative mortgage loan structure. John Harris, who had been in the business forty years and was someone Czelarc admired, was appreciative. "It took a young hot shot like you" – *hot shot*: that was the age Harris bridged forward from – "to understand there are thirteen ways of looking at a mortgage." Harris's partner had displayed a broad smile. "Don't you love a man," he said, turning toward Czelarc, "who knows his Wallace Stevens?" Czelarc had laughed particularly hard. That evening he went to the computer to learn the two men had been talking about poetry.

* * *

Sending an anonymous poem was a crazy thing, but hard times made people do crazy things. Even before the recession life in Phoenix bordered on the precarious. Czelarc had sold the homes with a slogan: "They'll Believe You Now." No one ever felt the need to ask what the slogan meant. If you lived in a neighborhood that was a reward, as Phoenix was, there couldn't be any question but that you'd made a success of things. People were often surprised when an acquaintance moved into Phoenix: how had they done it? It was Czelarc's ingenuity that snared his buyers. The mortgage rates were startlingly low – buyers looked long and hard at the term sheets and then still asked Czelarc to make sure they were reading the numbers right. The rates could be kept low because the mortgages themselves were complicated, running for unusually short spans of time, morphing in reaction to global rates Czelarc's new homeowners knew nothing about. Phoenix had filled up quickly. The Walkers had three children in college, but Czelarc nevertheless persuaded them to move into a home with more bedrooms than would ever be slept in. The Kellers' children, on the other hand, were young. "I have five and three" – five bedrooms, three baths – "a cabin, cars and trucks, boats, snowmobiles, and two hundred acres of hunting land," Travis Keller told Czelarc one evening, six months into Phoenix. "I'm living the American dream." He said this with irony, knowing that even a single missed paycheck would wake him.

Everything had fallen like dominoes, one thing knocking down another. Gasoline became expensive. Shoppers stopped shopping. The stock market tumbled and then came the lay-off notices. You looked out a window at the world and one day realized what you were seeing was a reflection: yourself, with all the familiar and pre-ordained limitations. The balloon dates Czelarc had engineered arrived. His buyers had no money to make the payments and the banks were too preoccupied with their own problems to help. Over a single weekend nine sale signs appeared on Phoenix lawns. The foreclosure notices added pages to the newspaper; not a few of the notices described Phoenix properties. Phoenix became still. The neighborhood had become a sort of purgatory, Czelarc realized: the mortgages he had designed and packaged and sold to the coasts were in their redemption periods.

Redemption period: it was a term few in Phoenix understood or had even heard, until now. Czelarc knew it – it was one of those terms that over twenty years had migrated from strange to recognizable to second nature, capable of being used without effort. Like parallels and meridians, which were the imaginary lines by which land – entire continents – was boxed into squares. It was a sloping globe, of course, meaning that those with an eye for detail understood that parallels and meridians would leave slivers no one would ever own. The Rule of 100, that was another part of the language. It was rudimentary – every landlord knew it. Multiplying monthly rent by one hundred would give you a rough idea of a property's value. The Rule of 100, like the idea of parallel and meridian slivers, was capable of being cast in a metaphysical light, if one were open to that sort of thinking. Multiply something as mundane as the monthly rent check and – *voila!* True value!

And *redemption period* had a lofty shimmer as well. Czelarc knew this but found any suggestion of the spiritual absurd. It was the sort of contrivance he had identified way back in college. If it was necessary to layer meanings onto business terms, Czelarc preferred the sexual to the spiritual. Wrap-around mortgages, piercings of the corporate veil – Czelarc had noted the connotations early. The men who invented the commercial world had been an aggressive bunch, Czelarc surmised.

A redemption period was in fact the span of time following a foreclosure sale. By law the homeowner was protected from eviction. There was no hope of selling the property and no obligation to make payments anymore. It was a lull, those months before the redemption period would abruptly end and the home – *home* – would be abandoned, by legal process or simple surrender. During the redemption period a family's lives were on hold: you were on the line, receiver to the ear, waiting, waiting. No plans could be made when you didn't know where you would next live or whether your children could remain in their school. As Phoenix calcified Czelarc grew gloomy over the drag on his development and, indeed, his reputation.

* * *

Semester Abroad

Upon her return she sees everything
for its wrongness: the little things
like yards not meters,
the big things like the Pentagon.
Her father and brother argue
about the National Basketball Association,
poor officiating, the utter idiocy
of a contemplated rule change.
Her mother wonders
about the rearrangement
of furniture. And school,
don't get her started: stupid
alcohol policies, spring dances, if you
can believe it, a pie-eating contest.
But she's touched, too, by the oddest things,
odd in having never been noticed
exactly this way before.

The warm brush on the cheek
of winter losing its grasp,
how each evening, after the cafeteria's
cheerless fare, the sky is brighter,
in a way her roommates don't see,
than yesterday's sky,
as though a flower were opening,
introducing itself, though anchored in earth,
to the world.

When the second poem arrived, ten days later, Czelarc opened the envelope as though knowing exactly what lay inside. No name was provided, as before; but Czelarc had no doubt "Semester Abroad" had been written and sent by the same person responsible for "Plans." Both poems were easy to understand – a girl got sick and missed her prom, a girl (the same girl, but older?) returned changed from studying abroad. What confounded Czelarc was the disclosure, the promiscuity. A daughter's bemusement – no, condescension – at her parents. A young woman's unexpressed thoughts. Who would broadcast this to a stranger? A parent wouldn't, but Czelarc was certain the poems had been written by a parent. Who but a parent would have known the things the poems knew? There was something else. These poems weren't written for him. *Sent* to him, yes, but the feel of the poems convinced Czelarc they weren't really about communication. It was more like talking to yourself, then wanting someone else (Czelarc) to know you were doing it. And the language – the way of looking at the world, really – was a different language, a different way. Slower and more careful. Smarter, perhaps: Czelarc didn't flinch from the thought. He respected her, this poet; but not as a parent.

A day or two later Czelarc, puzzling hard over this second poem, conceded that perhaps the poet *had* been the girl in the poem. Maybe she was a young mother – there were many in Phoenix, working long professional hours – recalling what life had been like in an earlier time. That the poems came from Phoenix was something Czelarc did not doubt. It was easy to imagine being blamed for the economic distress. One of his buyers wanted him to know there were faces behind the misery: wasn't that the motive? As though Czelarc needed reminding. He saw the yard signs and what they were doing to his development. He had heard his backers tell him there was no longer money available. It was hard times for Czelarc, too.

Czelarc found himself more attentive to the neighbors he saw mowing their lawns, walking their dogs, leaving Phoenix for work each morning. He reviewed his files and thought hard to recall each family that had bought into the subdivision. Were there daughters? Was there a professor or teacher (unlikely), someone capable of writing poems? Was there a retired grandparent (also unlikely, not in Phoenix's towering homes) with the time on her hands to daydream about such things? Over the past few years Czelarc had heard nothing of senior proms or semesters abroad, but then he actually spent little time in Phoenix – his days were passed downtown. Czelarc had a girlfriend in Colorado (introduced to him by his lawyer a year before), and the weekends he could get away found Czelarc on airplanes to and from Denver.

He became a better observer. It was amazing how much you could learn simply by watching the people behind you while you waited at the stoplight leaving Phoenix. From his rearview mirror Czelarc watched students sing with the radio as they left for school. He saw Olson (Czelarc was reasonably certain of the name) tie his tie, Hendrickson read his newspaper, Moe drink from a coffee cup big as a pail of ice cream. Couples were the most interesting. They talked without looking at one another, even with the car stopped, both staring straight ahead but smiling at what the other was saying. Laughing, too. At first it struck Czelarc as strange that there could be so much smiling and laughing while the stock market was tumbling hundreds of points each day. And people were not uniformly funny, either, in Czelarc's experience. It wasn't likely that jokes were being told – instead, these couples were probably working out who would pick up the dry cleaning and whether school conferences were on Wednesday or Thursday. Smiles, Czelarc began to realize, had little to do with funniness. Laughter didn't mean anything clever was being said. It was just another mode – *the* mode, possibly – of communication.

Czelarc's girlfriend became involved in a month-long trial and, the real estate industry having walked itself into a swamp, Czelarc found his weekends free. On a Saturday morning he put on running shoes and shorts and started down one of the paved trails that had been required as a condition of Phoenix's special use permit. It was a brilliant June morning and people were out. Some of the faces were familiar.

"I don't see *you* here often," a friendly voice called to Czelarc. Czelarc recalled the face but the name was elusive – Jeff, he thought. The two men stopped to talk about the morning and then the Twins before Czelarc said, abruptly, "Say, don't you have a college daughter?"

"My oldest," Jeff answered, and the thought of her widened his eyes and quickened his voice. "She just got home last week."

"She was traveling?"

"Home from school," Jeff corrected. "One year down, three to go, is what her mother says, but I can't even think about three to go. Heidi's first year has been more than enough by itself."

Czelarc wasn't sure what to make of this. His interest had been dampened by Jeff's clarification. Czelarc, who looked hard into the eyes while conducting business, began to admire the train of people appearing on the trail. They looked familiar in the way everyone living generally the same life looks familiar. They looked, Czelarc thought, like one another. "Someone was telling me how frequently college students go overseas these days," he said.

"Heidi's talking about it already. It's a wide open world to kids now. She wasn't gone a month before a boy painted her picture." Jeff smiled at the memory, still new. "Then she got her own show on the campus radio station. It was way off in the middle of the night. That's the shift the first-years get. Every Friday she set the alarm for three a.m. and then trudged across campus so she could spin records."

"Records don't spin anymore," Czelarc laughed, slapping Jeff's shoulder and starting on his way. "Which shows what you and I know."

Around the next bend Czelarc approached a woman he remembered from one of the dozens of closings over the past six years. She was the age to have teenage daughters, who of course would be friends with other girls.

"Julie, isn't it?" Czelarc greeted her.

The woman looked at Czelarc as though he might accost her. She crossed over to the other side of the asphalt and picked up speed.

Czelarc had been right: the woman's name was Julie. She and her husband Steve had bought into Phoenix four years earlier. Czelarc saw her sweeping the driveway a few days later, and the house address matched with the names in Czelarc's file for the property. A copy of an application indicated Steve and Julie had two teenage children – teenage plus four years, now. Later in the week Czelarc saw the entire family pass by in the car. Steve and Julie had sons.

* * *

In three more weeks the third poem arrived. Czelarc had told no one of the first two: the absurdity was more than an annoyance, it was an embarrassment. It was true that these envelopes brought with them the smallest flicker of danger, but danger was a spark immediately blanketed by the darkness of revulsion. Unsolicited poems, mailed anonymously – it *was* a schoolboy prank, even if the poems were not schoolboy efforts. It was silly, and made Czelarc appear silly. It was mocking. Someone was demeaning him.

Czelarc opened the third envelope and the first piece of paper he drew from it was empty. A blank sheet, sharply folded into three rectangular panels. The second sheet was the poem:

After a Child's Surgery

I would climb, those snowy mornings,
up from the floor, the corridor's
night shift darkness lifted.
You blinked ahead as though harnessed
by your tubes, fit with blinders,
angled just enough to suggest
a catapult soon to be sprung.
Mom arrived among the morning nurses
and I paced with excitement,
releasing to her our news, good
news, the night quiet but for
the morphine silliness – IVs as iPods,
you insisted, and were we ready
for caroling in our Disney costumes?
We laughed, Mom and I; you seemed
to smile. We were on the other side,
the day we had dreaded receding
like a failed life. An afterlife,
that is what it seemed,
happy as a child's Christmas,
all the natural laws suspended.

With Mom came yesterday's mail,
the cards, this or that
for breakfast. And the morning paper,
which I examined slowly, page by page,
finding it all newly interesting, though
having nothing to do with any of us,
really, any more.

Czelarc read the poem and then paced some, the sheet in his hand. Then he read it again. This was no prank, after all. He stuffed the poem into his desk but returned to it three more times that day. *Mom arrived among the morning nurses.* The poem was appalling, really, offering to a stranger's eyes the strongest emotions a parent could feel. *We were on the other side, the day we had dreaded receding like a failed life.* He was unstable, this person, this poet – Czelarc couldn't get the idea of instability out of his head. But the poem didn't make him, the poet, seem unstable.

The blank sheet tormented Czelarc. He was now waking often during the night – business was bad, very bad – but after thinking through the constipated real estate market his mind would turn to the blank sheet. It was an invitation, obviously. This poetry, you should try it: wasn't that what Czelarc was being told?

There was also a puzzle-piece aspect to all this. A picture was forming of a daughter, maybe two or three daughters – a whole daughterhood, Czelarc imagined – who had been in the operating room, missed the prom, been enlightened by Europe or Japan or South Africa. The poem affected Czelarc strongly; a week after its arrival he was still pulling it out of his desk each day. One evening, without knowing why, he began to copy this third poem onto the blank sheet of paper he had been provided. His idea may have been that *writing* the poem, rather than merely reading it, could open to him its possibilities, some hint, some clue. This was a trick he had learned in college, copying in longhand the most important passages from his marketing texts. As he copied the lines he became aware of a rhythm, a thumping that might have even been the coursing blood sounding in his ears. Then the thumping stopped, followed after a second or two by the jarring rattle of an errant shot banging off the basketball hoop's rim.

His name was Nicky McGough, this basketball boy. He was tall and thin, plagued by acne. Was it possible that Czelarc, two houses away, had never before seen him?

"Do I know you?" Czelarc said in his loud and friendly business voice. The rattle of the rim had made Czelarc toss down his pen, even before finishing the poem, and charge out into the warm twilight. He had approached Nicky with a big, purposeful stride. "I thought I knew everyone on this street."

Nicky held the ball. He knew Joe Czelarc. "Just shooting a few baskets," he said shyly.

"Your parents are Jim McGough." The name he remembered – Jim's, anyway – but he was unable to recall the faces.

"Susan's my mom." Nicky bounced the ball once and then held it again, warily.

"Someone was telling me about *someone* in the hospital. Someone in the neighborhood here, maybe a classmate of yours. What grade are you in?"

"Eleventh grade next year."

"Do you know what they could have been talking about? It was a surgery." Except in important situations, business situations, Czelarc wasn't often aware of how he was appearing in context; such things didn't carry much importance. But he knew now he was pushing hard on this boy, appearing unannounced with questions. Czelarc sensed he was near an answer, a mere two houses away and about to be disclosed by a boy shooting baskets in his driveway.

Nicky McGough looked at his shoes indifferently. "What kind of surgery?"

"They didn't say."

"That could be anybody, then. My friend Michael broke his leg playing football."

Czelarc took a step closer. "No, I'm pretty sure this was a girl."

"Well, then maybe it was one of the Rice girls. She had an infection last winter and missed school three weeks. Melissa Rice." Nicky thought a moment. "Or maybe Amy was the one. They're twins."

"Are they the ones with the older sister? In college?"

Uncomfortable with the attention, the boy gave a nervous laugh. "I have no idea," he said bravely. "There are a lot of kids in this neighborhood."

Yes, that was true: there *were* a lot of kids. The words stayed with Czelarc, first in Nicky McGough's voice and then in what Czelarc took to be a collective voice. Czelarc never thought of himself as fanciful, but the message he had received seemed to him a slogan, the neighborhood's own bouncing back at him. As summer deepened Czelarc challenged himself to learn who these people were. He began taking nightly walks with no purpose other than allowing him to spot and then greet Phoenix's residents. All these residents knew Czelarc. Some had nothing to say to him. Others were tentative, still others content to simply wave and smile. Nicky McGough's observation was confirmed: there was an abundance of sons and daughters. Czelarc no longer hoped to identify the characters in his three poems, or the poet. Anyone could have been the poem daughters: anyone *was* the poem daughters, Czelarc ventured. All of them were back from Cameroon, or waiting for next year's prom, or thinking of the hospital. Czelarc heard their stories – he heard a different story every night. He even heard stories in which he was the villain. Czelarc never received a fourth poem. The poems, like his neighbors, belonged to a month (or a few years) that was here and gone. The houses alone did not change; Czelarc's father had been right.

The Gentleness of Heaven

Great men are awarded long funerals, and it was four o'clock before Fred Black returned from the church and ascended the worn broad stairs. He scanned Friday afternoon's messages – rearrangements of his calendar, mostly, changes heralded in on squares of pink paper – before glancing up to see a boy and girl who had found their way through the back corridor. Conversation between Black and the boy began haltingly, each cautious of the other's imagined advantage. The girl remained silent, occasionally brushing back her hair with a sweeping motion of counterfeited indifference. All had papers to assist their maneuverings. After forty minutes the children left and, by agreement, they and Black gathered again the following noon.

By then the heat was accumulating upon Wheeling steadily, like water filling a tank. Over the past week spring had given way to unprecedented torpor. Isolated sounds, here then gone, predominated: the growls of the long cylindrical tanker trucks climbing through their gears along the surrender of Atlantic Street; the band saw shrieks of water glancing off silver circles embedded in black rubber like knots in timber; the clapping violence of metal doors flung shut. The children who had emerged from those doors held flowers and long bright clothing.

Air conditioning cooled the Goetz house, but the cavernous garage, emptied of its vehicles to make room for the tables – emptied of trucks, motorcycles, four-wheelers, a boat on a trailer – held eddies of rank air not reached by the floor fans. Peter looked past his cousins, scavenging from a memorized list. A spare wrench, large screwdriver, pair of pliers; a flashlight and burlap bag of discarded silverware and cooking utensils once used for camping; after a moment's hesitation, a short snow shovel, not on the list but indispensable during the past winter. This was the last of the surreptitious rounds, bedroom to basement to garage, that had begun as early as Easter weekend – the thrill still burned strong in Peter – and accelerated upon August Goetz's death.

"Kissy kissy," squealed Teddy.

"Keep your voice down," said Belinda severely. *Her* voice, though, was not quiet, and sounded like a coil of barbed wire scraping down an alleyway.

"Kissy kissy," Teddy said in a chastened voice. "Aunt Belinda, did you ever go to dances?"

"Aren't you hot, Teddy? Silence will keep you cooler."

"I couldn't dance," cried Janie. "Not tonight. I'd think of Great Grandpa."

"I'd see his face!"

Peter's thoughts were elsewhere. With Elise, certainly, who was experiencing her own adventures; but also with Peter's uncle, an impulsive man whose break with the family had occurred before Peter had been born. And with all the silly busyness ahead, the costumes and paper streamers and awkward formality and his speech. Silly, but still important to Peter, if not to Elise. The guests who had settled in for the weekend – a hundred of them, all the sisters and brothers (except Hank) of Peter's father, and all their children, the extended families, an entire constellation folding out from the tip of the spear, now dark – these guests were not important to Peter. But he was grateful for their presence.

Elise was alone when Peter arrived shortly before six. The house was shabby, its calamine shakes cracked and occasionally absent, winter's soiled cardboard and ridges of pebbles not yet cleared from the yard. Elise emerged wearing a soft yellow dress, modest and clumsily cut. In her face – in her eyes, Peter often thought, and down across her soft cheeks – was a steadfastness. She had no panic point. Peter had noticed this as long ago as eighth grade. They had visited an arcade the evening before

Thanksgiving, four and a half years earlier: their own creation story. Elise, a controlled smile on her lips, pulled herself up into the pickup and looked out the windshield, avoiding Peter's eyes. Peter had wondered how she would treat this moment.

Many of the couples entered the school in sixes and eights, but Peter and Elise walked in alone. The heat had been slow to leave the auditorium floor, and already some of the boys had removed their jackets and draped them over the opened metal chairs. This was where much of school life took place – assemblies, plays, basketball games, now the spring prom – and a poignancy unexpectedly tightened Peter's throat. In two weekends he would walk into this auditorium for graduation ceremonies; and then never enter again. For the truth, despite the pinch of memory, was that he had merely endured his years here. The teachers had been fools, their classes insulting, the entire culture one of nurtured complacency. Peter put none of the blame on his classmates: they had simply filled the form they'd been poured into. But Wheeling High School was a creation of Wheeling itself, and Peter had for the past two years counted the weeks remaining before his departure. "I'll never come back," he had told Elise. She hadn't wanted to come back either.

The evening would combine a dinner with a program that Peter, by virtue of his office, had a part in; and then the tables would be collapsed, the chairs pushed to the perimeter, and the lights lowered for a dance orchestrated by a rented disc jockey. Peter and Elise sat with five other couples at a head table. Elise ate contentedly but in silence, smiling occasionally at one of Peter's overheard jokes. Though having lived her entire life in Wheeling, her native reserve and long attachment to Peter had kept her virtually friendless among the school's girls. But Peter was a great favorite, admired for none of the usual reasons. Though tall and muscular, he disdained athletics. He was more interested in learning than was any other Wheeling student; he was more interested in learning than the teachers were in teaching. His ambition was charmingly guileless, and his sheer recklessness – as a sophomore he had angrily corrected the biology teacher half a dozen times during a single lecture on cell division – made him irresistible to the other boys. He was moody, but when not troubled had a generous laugh that Peter's classmates sought as a sign of his approval. He was the best Wheeling student of his generation.

But Peter's speech, a mix of invented awards and senior class anecdotes, fell flat. On another night Peter might have veered toward an unguarded weirdness his classmates would have recognized and appreciated, but on this night a philosophical, almost nostalgic, thread appeared to Peter and he followed to where it led. Except that it led nowhere – Peter hadn't thought out the conclusion, and after five minutes his talk simply trailed away.

The dance began and the folding chair to Peter's left was immediately taken by Jason Burleson. Jason saw that Peter was in high excitement, eyes darting around the room and his words to Elise firing in rapid bursts, chaotic as hail caroming off pavement. A break in the conversation occurred without notice and Jason, searching his friend's face intently, blurted out: "Peter?" He had intended to laugh but in fact a panic squeezed his face. Peter steadied himself in preparation. "My sister keeps calendar for Fred Black."

"Good old Fred Black."

"Was this your idea?"

Peter laughed aggressively. "You looked at her stomach when you said that."

This drew Elise into the conversation. "Nice jacket," she smiled. Peter's friends were her friends.

Jason glanced down absent-mindedly at the lime lapel. "Hey, Elise." Then, courageously: "This feels like the end of something, you two."

Peter regarded Jason's observation thoughtfully. "Thank God," Elise murmured.

"Where will you live?"

"On Atlantic. My uncle has a building."

The enormity of the idea silenced Jason. He looked away

to think. A fraction of the students were wriggling in the dance floor shadows and a fraction were, like the three of them, seated in the chairs surrounding the cleared gymnasium floor. The others had moved out of the room and were loudly circulating through the bright hallway that wrapped itself around the auditorium.

"Were you thinking of this all along?" Grievance introduced itself before being swamped under by a disbelieving admiration. "Last fall at the quarry, for instance. Had you planned it by then?"

Peter yielded to the question, reconstructing the soft September Friday evening. He and Elise, Jason and a since-forgotten Michelle, had retreated from the homecoming game into the bluffs. They had drank a sugary wine and watched the burning ring of stadium lights in the valley below.

"I don't know," he said, the slightest dismay crossing his face. "Had we, Elise?"

Elise gave a sly smile, slowly forming. "Of course we had."

Jason regarded her smile as a signal. "Married!" he said to Peter in astonishment.

"Married."

"There's no changing your mind now."

"No," Peter smiled.

"I mean, you're married already, right as we're talking."

Elise giggled. "We're granting you a portion of our wedding night, Jason."

Though protected by the dimmed lights, Jason fought unsuccessfully to keep his freckles from reddening. He looked hard at Peter, eyes stretched into circles. Waiting.

"It's a rush. I couldn't have imagined."

A bearded man moved with the caution of the afflicted into one of the doorways leading out of the auditorium. His silhouette caught Peter's eye; Peter touched Elise's thigh as a reassurance and left her, approaching his uncle in long strides. "Don't look so worried," he said in greeting, though he himself was uneasy at Hank's sudden appearance. Couples in the vicinity stopped to overhear.

"Have you seen your father?" Hank shifted his weight stiffly. "He stopped at the house tonight."

"Which he wouldn't usually do."

"No. But he said Dad's death should make us rethink." Hank betrayed no judgment. He looked at the gathering crowd and nodded toward the emptiness at the end of the hallway. "Pam told him about you and Elise seeing the judge this morning."

"Why would she do that?"

"It was hard for her to bear, the thought of him not even knowing about his own son's wedding." A traitorous hip forced Hank to walk with the rhythm of a carnival engine, his shoulders rising and falling in great effort, Peter easily imaging the *doong, che doong, che doong.* "You can't fault her for that."

"No."

"But all the same, he may be up here looking for you two."

They moved beyond the students to the smoked classroom windows that Peter knew so well and Hank remembered from a generation earlier. "There's a smell these halls get in warm weather. Whatever it is, it's never changed."

"We were sure the distraction of Grandpa's funeral and all the guests would at least get us through the weekend. The distraction of prom, too. It was Elise's idea not to wait. It seemed like the perfect opportunity."

"Pam didn't tell him about the apartment. She thought he'll find out soon enough. And you deserve at least the weekend unmolested. She told your father you two must have left town. But he might find his way up here, looking for some answers."

Peter's father had achieved his fearsome position – Goetz Oil Transportation was his, a fleet of trucks and drivers, Wheeling's link between the refineries and the diesel stations – by expecting answers. And by being August's son, of course, Peter's father in many ways being less impressive than the man whose long illness and death had been genuinely grieved throughout the valley. "He'll want to know why we couldn't wait," Peter said, knowing that what his father would really wonder was whether Peter was trying to prove something. To spite someone. Why else would he preemptively surrender all those years, so many other women, without knowing what he was surrendering? It was something Charlie Goetz couldn't imagine.

Hank started for the truck he had left in the school lot and Peter threaded his way back to Elise. The astounding news had lit the auditorium, the students following the story like flowers turning with the climbing sun. Their little world – high school corridors, Wheeling in its decades-long decline – had been realigned: the class president had married. Other students had married, of course, two or three couples each year, but they had been preparing for babies and none ever finished school. None spoke of medical school.

Elise was no longer talking with Jason; she had instead moved across the room and when Peter found her, after anxious minutes of hard searching, she was seated next to Molly Lacklyn, a girl Peter hadn't seen her speak with since early in the school year. Now, mysteriously, they were laughing.

"The clock's ringing twelve," Peter said. "The spell of prom is over."

Elise heard the urgency. She rose matter-of-factly – alarm was outside her range of emotions – and started with Peter for the hallway. Their classmates watched but said nothing. "Stymied," Elise quietly observed for Peter with a smile.

But Ms. McGordy, who had arrived in Wheeling four years earlier as the high school's assistant principal, was not stymied. She approached rapidly once Peter and Elise closed in on the double doors through which Hank had left. Peter slowed. "No," Elise said firmly. Peter, she knew, respected Ms. McGordy; he was vulnerable.

"Do your parents know about this?" McGordy demanded. Her large face was made white by the smolder of thick auburn hair. She was young, hardly twenty years out of school herself. "My God."

"*No,*" Elise said in a sharp whisper. She gave Peter an

angry look; walking now more quickly, she continued alone toward the door.

"My parents? They've had a lot on their minds this week."

McGordy's eyes narrowed as though she had just heard the manufacture of a sick pet to justify a skipped day of school. "That's disingenuous," she said, offended.

"But the great thing about being an adult," Peter said in a reasonable voice, "is that now I don't owe anyone any explanations."

This wounded McGordy. "You can't talk to me like that. I've known you since the day I got here. Since your voice was squeaking in the treble clef."

"But it's true."

"You're still a student, though, Peter. Aren't you? For ten more days?"

Peter's lips curled into an exasperated smile. "I'll be a student for ten more years, Ms. McGordy."

"But how can you?"

"We're moving into student housing the end of August. Down in Chicago."

"Money?" the principal said, fighting defeat.

Peter turned toward the door. "I'll stop in to talk after school Monday." He smiled, supremely confident. "Spending your senior prom in conversation with the principal – how lame is that?"

"What *about* that?" Ms. McGordy cried in afterthought. "What in the world are you doing here? Tonight!" The mistake in judgment proved the tragedy of his miscalculation.

"For the same reason everyone else is here. We're still students. Except that we want to be married."

Elise, about whom McGordy hadn't asked, was waiting in the dark pickup. The day's heat had given way to a vast stillness, improbably punctuated by sweeps of wind running through the new leaves on the high branches. The small, distant sounds of early afternoon – Peter was certain he would never forget the details of the slow drive from the courthouse, bringing Elise back, one last time, to an indifferent family – had been replaced by night sounds, also distant and unexpectedly clear. A child's giggle. Twenty thousand voices of unhurried encouragement, delivered from a remote ballyard and filtered through a single unseen radio.

"No sign of trouble?" Peter said, climbing in beside Elise. He removed his jacket and laid it carefully behind him.

"Not a Charlie Goetz to be seen. Hank's not here, either, but he left these." Somberness broke into a broad smile as she lifted her bare arm and dangled their apartment keys.

The anxiety that had possessed Elise inside the school was evidently gone also. Perhaps, Peter considered, it would be characteristic of Elise to rebound quickly from anger. He could recall fighting with her but once. During the spring of their junior year a class trip had taken them to Chicago for a four-day weekend. They were together each day from breakfast until past midnight, standing on the hard museum floors, waiting in roped lines, stuck once for an hour and a half in a bus that had broken down near the Water Tower. When a replacement finally arrived, pulling up to the opposite curb, the class had pushed its way out of the bus and darted blindly into four lanes of intermittent traffic. During the wait Elise had glared with unhappiness – Peter could not recall what exactly had been the reason, beyond too much time with too many classmates. She followed him silently out of the bus, refusing to respond to his transparent small talk. Peter rounded the corner of their abandoned bus and saw in a glance a car approaching down the near lane at forty miles per hour. He almost didn't raise his arm to prevent Elise, following hard behind, from stepping in front of the car that would have killed her. His instinct, preceding thought, had been to avoid the violation of touch. And his instinct had been right: during the flicker of time after running forcefully into Peter's outstretched arm, but before apprehending what had happened, Elise's eyes flashed outrage. Just as easily Peter could have kept his body to himself. Chance alone had saved them.

The drive to their new home – five miles of stoplights past abandoned buildings and vacant lots, the night shift and bar traffic of Atlantic Street – was solemn. Elise spoke in whispers. Peter parked his truck in the small gravel lot behind his uncle's solitary brick building, tall and narrow with its empty storefront below and two apartments above. Peter used his keys – Elise's were duplicates, given by Hank in ritual – and opened the locks on a metal door that led to a steep flight of stairs, then another, turning on landings and echoing as though Peter and Elise were stepping across the tops of empty wooden boxes. A bulb curling down from the high ceiling glowed yellow against the smudged walls, milky green, but left the corners in shadows. Off the second landing a hole the size of a boot exposed the sticks behind the plaster.

The fluorescent light in their apartment entrance flickered on in stages a moment after Peter snapped the switch up loudly. "Thank you, Hank," Peter said: a fan had been lodged in one of the front windows and the motor was working furiously. On Peter's right was a doorway leading to the bathroom, on his left a stove and a refrigerator he had stocked with a bag of groceries just that afternoon, during the last of a handful of trips he had made to the apartment over the past month. Beyond the linoleum the apartment opened into a larger room arranged as two. In front of one window sat a dark circular table with thick legs stretching into monstrous paws; and before the other was a small television on a stand with casters and, back against the wall, a double bed. "Home," Peter said.

The apartment had captured the day's ferocious heat. Peter opened the freezer and a small cloud of cool, dry air emerged tentatively. "Try this," he said to Elise, crowding close to the dark, rectangular opening. Then, with enthusiasm: "And this. I made them this afternoon." Two small cups of chocolate milk had frozen into wedding treats; gently curving spoon handles sprouted upward toward the ice crystals clustered on the freezer ceiling.

Elise, her face a deep red, had moved in front of the fan. She pulled her dress off in one great motion, dumping it to the floor. Her damp slip followed. Peter watched carefully, studying the strangeness of female construction, legs running high up the sides of her torso, the moon of her belly low and fleshy, its ring softening into an expanse of hips. He and Elise had made love before, though just often enough to be unable to recall a precise number. A wildness took possession of Elise's face. Dragging the dress beside her, she pushed the television cart aside, crouched low to leverage open the screen, and stuffed the dress, segment by segment, through the window and into the night. "Take that," she said. A bead of sweat trickled down erratically from beneath her arm.

Peter was amazed. He arrived at the window in time to see the dress drape itself softly upon the corner fire hydrant. Elise waited for his response, but Peter only stared down in wonder. "Look at that," he finally said when the dress rippled in the wake of a passing truck. "Hadn't you worked so hard?" He was tremendously happy. No one else in his entire world would have done such a thing.

The freezer door remained open. When Elise closed it she also switched off the apartment's light and moved one of the chairs from the table to the window. Peter edged into the chair and Elise followed, shifting to make herself comfortable in his lap. They looked up and down Atlantic Street, observing the long arms of the light standards and absorbing the hum of the transformers. Another truck passed – they all ran the same direction, south toward the interstate – and the exchange of acceleration and ascending gears was audible for miles.

In dawn's imprecision Elise woke to a burst of patter from behind the wall. A gray curtain of sky filled the near window. Rain was falling steadily and from the distance Elise heard the prolonged rumble of soft parting thunder. Peter was at the table, wearing a T-shirt and sweats and peering through the grainy light at a book that Elise knew, from its size, to be his chemistry text. The window fan was quiet.

"Did you know Uncle Hank has mice?" she said sleepily.

"Do you think he let them in to remind me of home?"

Peter acknowledged her with a bob of his head but didn't look up. The bed's springs gave a ragged swallowing sound as Elise swung her legs out from under the sheet she had gathered around herself during the night. Her feet adhered lightly to the floor, gently slapping as she walked to the window to evaluate the morning. The rain slowed its drum across the rooftop.

"Peter," she said, startled. "Look what's happening to my dress!"

Though curious, Peter kept his eyes on the page while rising to join Elise at the window. Below, on a sidewalk darkened by rain, a boy both knew from school was holding Elise's dress up for inspection.

"Mr. Paperboy!" Elise called cheerfully. Fully awake, she began to giggle as the boy looked up and down the street. "No, up here."

"What's the world like this morning, Tom?" Peter said. A deep, worn bag, heavy with Sunday's news, was strapped over Tom's shoulders.

Tom labored to place the faces pressed against the screen overhead. Life's winnowing had separated him from most of his classmates following sixth grade; a few years later, newspaper delivery had taken school's place. "Is that you, Peter?" he said timidly.

"And me, Elise Peterson. Elise *Goetz*. We're married, Tom!"

Tom stood transfixed, mouth open. He let the yellow dress slip from his fingers. "Both of you?"

Their laughter momentarily frightened him, but alarm was followed quickly by wariness, then curiosity. Finally, taking the laughter as permission, Tom broke into a wide smile.

"Both of us!" said Peter.

"Both of you!" Tom agreed triumphantly. Hitching the bag high on his shoulder, he shook his head in satisfaction and started off down the walk, his laughter punching in small explosions against the waning drizzle.

There Is No Sadness

My grandfather pitched one season for the Philadelphia Athletics.
The only story he ever told me, until much later, was about the
time he hit Babe Ruth on the foot with a pitch. Ruth howled
and took a step toward Grandpa. But they were in Philadelphia.
Ruth muttered something, flipped the bat over his shoulder, and
broke into a grin. He walked down to first base. "It was all those
circles that protected me," Grandpa said. By this he meant the
ring of his infielders, inside the ring of his outfielders, inside
the ring of the stadium. All those circumscriptions saved him,
was his view.

I should have asked him so many questions. I know that
now. In those days ballplayers were like circus performers or
vaudevillians. I've read that Gabby Street, on a bet, caught a
ball dropped from the top of the Washington Monument. Hans
Lobert raced a horse around the bases. The ballplayers must
have often gone to the track. Once Germany Schaefer, not a
good hitter, announced to the crowd that he would hit a home
run. Which he did on the second pitch. He was so excited that
he slid into first, then second, then third and home, all the
while loudly describing his trip around the bases as though he
were not only the racehorse but the track announcer as well.

My mother was Grandpa Leo's daughter, and the four
of us – Grandpa, my parents, and I – lived in a stucco house a
short distance from Lake Mille Lacs. Grandpa had been born in
a farmhouse, since burned, a few miles down toward Ogilvie. No
one was aware of any other big leaguer from central Minnesota,
and Grandpa was a celebrity in a small town way. He was quiet
about it. When pressed he would make use of his Babe Ruth story,

the way a navy veteran might gamely roll up his sleeve to display an anchor from the South Pacific. In the warm months Grandpa fished early in the morning. By nine o'clock he had shuffled from the dock to the Miller Cafe for breakfast. Several of his friends roosted at the Miller all morning, like boys my father might have kept after class. Grandpa enjoyed listening to them, but after an hour he would leave for home and spend the rest of the day puttering around the garage and in the garden. He napped an hour each afternoon and joined us for supper before retiring early.

Dad had built Grandpa's bedroom off the living room. That happened during the summer between my seventh and eighth grade years, and then Grandpa had moved in that fall. Summer was when my father was happiest. Once the school year began he became quiet, sinking into himself as the autumn deepened, fully silent through winter and until spring startled us like a sigh from an open casket. The students wore him down. Math was solid; he never lost his admiration for math. But the students wore him down.

Dad's withdrawal seemed not to bother Mom, who had her poetry. She wrote five minutes here, five minutes there. She wrote in a florid, cloth-bound notebook Dad had bought her one summer in a gift shop up the North Shore. When an observation caught her away from her notebook – at the credit union, for example – she made use of whatever scrap of paper was available and then transferred the new phrase into her notebook that evening. It was not unusual to find pink phone messages littering the house, waiting to be transferred. "The pines in high wind don't sway in unison," I remember once reading, "but knock heads, like people." This told me she had had a particularly hard day at work. Or: "There is no sadness" – this was written after Grandpa returned from North Memorial – "like the sadness of someone you love."

Most of the poetry was rhymed. This was the problem. Poems departed and then returned home. Mom was forever typing the poems on her candy blue electric, inserting small white strips to correct errors. She was mailing envelopes to New York, Vermont, Georgia, Oklahoma, Idaho, each aimed at an oddly-named pamphlet – *Caramel Apple*, I remember, and there was a *Burning River* – identified in a thousand-page poets' guide Mom seemed to have on permanent loan from the library. She kept copies of everything, the poems and their letters of introduction. For a time she asked my father to help with the school's copier, but when he balked she made do with the copier in the back corner at Ben Franklin. She need not have bothered. No one valued rhymed poetry, and all the poems found their way back as surely as spring's robins. Mom gave a few to Bonita Thompson, whose family owned the newspaper. The poems were published and everyone in town read them – no one knew of, much less read, *Burning River* – and in this way Mom became known as a poet.

In late May of 1979, my junior year behind me, I returned for my last summer at home. The unpainted cabins and tunneled lawns of Meier's Resort awaited me. Earl and I – Earl, seventy and Swedish, excitable and nearly deaf, had been with Meier a decade or more – began by dropping ourselves into waders and sliding the docks back into Mille Lacs's black waters. The ice had been off less than a month.

"Down, down, down, way down," I said.

"What? Nooo!" That was Earl's response to those noises that made it over the moat and into his consciousness. *What?* meant he recognized the sound; *Nooo!* was his attempt to bluff comprehension. He was showing astonishment at your news. Whatever that news might be.

"Way down, Earl." Earl's loyal companion, with his thermos, was a radio he could not hear. The radio gave us farm reports in the morning, fishing reports at noon, funeral notices near quitting time. Between the talking there was country music – "Don Juan," "Heaven's Just a Sin Away," "There Ain't No Good Chain Gang" – that may or may not have been designed to elicit a smile. There were also many commercials. "We mark 'em down, down, down, way down," sang a barbershop bass on behalf of the hardware store in town.

> They're the very best prices around
> Come in and see us today
> We only mark 'em one way
> We mark 'em down   way
>   down
>   down
>   down.

"What?" Earl said a few weeks later, after the sirens had wailed a full minute. We were on our stomachs, spraying foam into mouse holes.

"Fire," I said. "Or ambulance."

"Nooo!"

Ambulance was right. White and boxy, it appeared across the bay on a quarter mile of highway that followed the shore. It moved slowly, in the way of ambulances, eventually turning from the lake and toward the hospital. The morning sun twinkled off the jumping watertop.

In a small town people come at such a story from all sides, listening and guessing and reasoning until they have something that can be explained and accepted. First we heard that Mel Toominen had fallen off one of the large lake homes up the shore. Mel Toominen was a roofer. Then we heard that it hadn't been Mel at all. And it hadn't been a fall, but a heart attack suffered by one of the cabin owners while pulling shingles. The word in town was that he had rolled off the roof. This had been picked up at the grocery store by a Nebraska man newly arrived to the resort.

Four new families arrived at Meier's Resort that morning. From a conversation across the lawn I heard the word *pitcher* – distant, then sudden as an odor carried in on the wind – and knew it had been Grandpa Leo inside that ambulance. The life drained from me. I felt fear and grief and abandonment and betrayal, but those words are only words and do not adequately describe the death I was dying. I walked out onto a dock, not to think but to escape the news. No one came for me until Meier himself came to tell me my father was on the telephone.

Grandpa had been helping his friend Walter. They had indeed been tearing shingles from a roof. Even at seventy-nine it was only a little unusual for Grandpa to be doing such a thing. Walter's garage was built into the side of a hill. Grandpa and Walter had been able to step up onto the roof without a ladder, but the shingles had become green with moss from years of wet dropping leaves. Grandpa had slid on his way down. He probably hit his head on the roof's edge; Walter had been inside the garage and had only heard the sudden noise overhead – it sounded like grackles swooping in fall, was the way he told it to the ambulance driver – before finding Grandpa's body beside the firewood stacked against the short back wall.

I learned all of this late the next day, when Dad returned. He and Mom had been called to the hospital and then had followed the ambulance when the emergency room nurse had sent it on down to Minneapolis. Dad's call to the resort had been made just before he and Mom left town. By staying behind I had made the most obvious of mistakes. The house's emptiness that evening forced me to acknowledge the capitulations required by our world as it had been recast. Life had changed – so fast it had changed – and there was no one to try and tell me otherwise. But I could not have gone to North Memorial. I imagined the part of me not flesh and bones – life force seemed a good name, or soul, maybe, or courage – and I saw it as the metal workings, barely visible, inside a watch. Grandpa's fall was a magnet carelessly introduced.

In the morning I rode with Dad back down to the hospital. I was led to intensive care, where Mom was sitting motionlessly in the far corner of the room closest to the nurses' station. There was nothing in the room to occupy Mom – not a book, magazine, or knitting needle; not her notebook – and this was the third day. Grandpa looked like something caught in a fisherman's net. Lines ran to and from him, fluids in and fluids out. Dad had tried to prepare me, but had said nothing about the restlessness. Grandpa rolled, as best the restraints allowed, from side to side. His moaning, too, was restricted. From the other side of the ventilator we heard, though muffled, the sound of violence. It was a heavy vacuum cleaner we heard, bruising its way down uncarpeted stairs.

Grandpa suffered and we suffered also. To me there was no distinction between physical pain and the anguish. If my essence was an intricate arrangement of tiny mechanisms that had been swept clean, my nervous system, I imagined, was a series of small curling coils being pulled straight. Wide bands tightened against my chest. When the phone rang each night – I had returned home, but Mom and Dad stayed at the hospital as one week drained into another – I backed away from the expected news. At times I felt anger, but mostly the anger was saving itself up.

Earl worked away in his soundless world and I, beside him, spent the days constructing a reason. Life is valuable, was my starting point. Something as trivial as the sweep of wind off the lake – the white, jagged-winged gulls fighting their way out and then sailing back on the gale, boomerangs – sufficiently proved the point. Valuable? Life is *everything*; literally, the only thing. The prospect of losing it is unbearable, more unbearable even than the actual loss. And so as our years progress we are besieged, crisis upon crisis, all to persuade us that life is not in fact so precious a thing. Its inevitable loss can be accepted. Humans, properly prepared, have that capacity. The logic fortified me. I understood life as a process of deflation. The syllable itself – *life* – was a deflation. The riddle was that something so punishing could be held so desperately.

After nineteen days Grandpa's eyes were opened. He began to speak. It was a Sunday and I, accompanying Mom and Dad, saw and heard it myself. Grandpa remembered nothing of Walter's garage and didn't answer when we asked about the past three weeks. Otherwise he was Grandpa. Knocked flat and stunned by the enormity of his struggle, but Grandpa.

"You're back, Dad," said Mom, late that day. She stroked the shoulder of his hospital gown.

"Back in there pitching," Grandpa replied. We were thrilled by the nuance of those four words, the balance between gratitude and humor and love.

The doctors gave us their warnings. We understood, but we had also been in the room when Grandpa had been given back to us. In a week Grandpa began to make trips to physical therapy. In three more weeks he came home. We guided him into his bedroom to begin a long convalescence. The four of us, not understanding the place we had been, were a family once more.

August arrived and darkness began to eat at the edges of the day. We told each other that we remembered this from earlier Augusts, and in this way reassured one another that we were living a circle, that Grandpa could in fact return. He rarely left his room. I came through the door at the end of each afternoon and found him in bed. He changed my personality. To fight off the fear I tried to engage Grandpa. I made a point of bringing home a joke each day. Sometimes the joke cheered him, but even when it didn't the distraction was a victory. In the mornings I said goodbye and sometimes detected slippage in his condition. The observation would set me back. All day I would examine the slippage the way a person examines any other wound. I probed it, worsened it. Then at four o'clock I came home with my joke. Sometimes Grandpa joined us for dinner, sometimes not. The best part of the day, I refused to admit, was when he closed his door for the night and the suffering was removed from our view.

Two weeks before summer's end I found Grandpa in his chair. "A duck walked into a bar," I said. It was Friday night and Mom would be at the credit union until seven. Dad was helping Mr. Rusk, the other math teacher, build a deck. "'One grape, please,' he said. The bartender says, 'This is a bar. We serve beer. We serve whiskey. We don't serve grapes.' So the duck left."

Grandpa's eyes were on his slippers. Even in the August heat – a window air conditioning unit ground away ineffectively from the far side of the living room – Grandpa wore a bathrobe over his heavy pajamas.

"The next day the duck comes back. 'One grape, please,' he says."

I watched in vain for a smile to form. Grandpa, eyes still downcast, waved at the bedroom's other chair as though shooing away a sand bee. "Sit down, Phil."

"So the bartender says, 'Listen, bird brain, I told you yesterday, I'll tell you today. This is a bar. We have beer, we have whiskey, we don't have grapes. If you ask one more time for a grape I'll nail your beak to the bar.' The duck turns around and walks out." I pulled the open chair close and sat down. Grandpa began to raise his eyes. "The next day," I said, "the duck comes back."

"I'm surprised," Grandpa said slowly, sensing trouble.

"'One nail, please,' he says."

"Nail?" Grandpa asked.

I nodded. "'One nail, please.' The bartender says, 'Nail? I don't have a nail.' 'Okay, then,' the duck says. 'One grape, please.'"

Grandpa smiled in appreciation. His teeth, long as pulled teeth, gave his head a skeletal look. "I don't know where you get these jokes," he said. "What is it you did all today?"

"Acted as though I understood how to fix an outboard motor. Listened to a lot of what noing from Earl."

Grandpa thought a moment. "Bars, you know, I went ten years without stepping foot in one. Not many ballplayers could say that."

Color had returned to his face. There were signs of improvement. But the color was garish, as though Grandpa had taken to makeup. His lips were red like a woman's.

"You see, I was at a bar on a train in Cuba when the train ran off the tracks. It wasn't much of a bar. But I could never go back. I got thrown right out a window or a door, something. I ended up down the hill, in swamp water. Seven ballplayers were killed."

"When was this?" It was a story I had never heard.

"November 29, 1923. My arm was broke but it wasn't my pitching arm. I was ready by next spring."

"How did it happen?"

Grandpa shrugged. "It was Cuba. I hit my head, too. When I woke up, still no one had come. I heard people screaming. I don't know how long I was in that water.

"When I played we talked a little about God. Not much, but it would come up." Grandpa's words came slowly, silence bookending each sentence. "I've wondered if that sort of thing gets discussed at a college." He looked up. "Does it?"

"What do you mean, exactly?"

Grandpa's neck stiffened in concentration. His skin was the slightest of drapery, thin as the silver on a fish.

"That's a big question, God. Intelligent people have points of view on it, I'm sure. That's what I would expect, anyway." His eyes had dropped but now he looked up again for confirmation. "Phil, do your classmates talk about this? Or your professors? Do you read books about such things?"

"Sure." But I was a business major and had never read such a book.

"What does everyone say?"

"Everyone has a different opinion, Grandpa."

"What is *your* opinion?"

"There are a lot of wonderful things in this world," I said, and then gave one of the speeches I had tried out, and rejected – never imagining it would be spoken – while working at Earl's side. "It's hard to believe they all got here by chance. So there's a force out there. Religion has its name for that force, but maybe it's enough to just say there's a force for *goodness.*"

Grandpa Leo said nothing. His lips moved the way a small boy's move when he is learning to read. "I've always believed in heaven," he finally said. "Like you, I've believed there is a force for goodness. That's a good way of saying it." I nodded cautiously. Grandpa kept his eyes away from me, as though acknowledgement would break his line of thought. "I don't know much about God. The Bible is an old book. I've often thought that for many people that old book has *become* their God. Life can be wonderful, as you say. When it is, we get an idea of heaven. I've often thought that."

He looked up sharply. "I've never believed God interferes with us. And I've never believed in judgment. A heaven for good people and a hell for bad – that's exactly what you'd expect humans to dream up. But a God wouldn't think that way.

"Down in that hospital" – he motioned with his head as though North Memorial were down the street – "I lived that train wreck. Dozens of times. *Hundreds* of times." Grandpa looked up at me in bewilderment. "It was a nightmare I couldn't get out of. And everything was confused, like it is in a nightmare. I kept calling for your mother. But she hadn't been born yet, you see." His voice tipped with the suddenness of a canoe. "I couldn't find her." Grandpa stilled himself and then his voice came back quiet. "And all the screaming," he said.

"You found a way to work yourself out of it."

"I never believed in hell," he continued. "That's because I couldn't imagine it. But it exists. The only way I could say it doesn't is to pretend those three weeks never happened."

He said most of this while staring at something I couldn't see. He doesn't need a listener, I thought; but just then he turned to me and asked, with headstrong curiosity: "Do you suppose, Phil, that when we die it's hell that waits for us? Not as a punishment, but as . . . ." He searched, not for a word, I was sure, but for a way of thinking about so big an idea. "As the next thing, the final thing? So that *hell* isn't even the right word for it. It's just what's *intended* for us."

"But Grandpa," I said.

"Have you ever heard of anyone who has thought about this possibility? Thought *hard* about it?"

I saw him tremble and resolved to say nothing – and what would I have said? – until he calmed himself. Grandpa's shoulders began to drop. His fingers moved toward his face, an ear, the back of his neck. They returned to his lap like birds returning to a line after approaching, and then fleeing, a plundered nest.

"There is no way of knowing, is there," he said. "I hope I'm misunderstanding. It's very hard to think of helplessness. In even the deepest suffering there are consolations. Knowing that there will be an end to the suffering would be a consolation. Time can provide a consolation. But *this*" – he twisted the word in outrage – "can provide no hope of consolation."

Grandpa stood up suddenly, as though the chair and his thoughts were one, and could be left behind. He walked over to the bed in the careful way his injury had taught him. Leaning gently against the mattress, he turned back and said, to be certain I understood, "I'm not talking about dying, Phil. What I'm talking about is something else. You know that."

One of Mom's poems included this couplet: "When the shadow of a cloud flies down a field / In the shadow, not the sun, is the field's truth revealed." I found this poem near the washing machine, Labor Day weekend, and knew the rhymes would keep it from publication. I was in the final stages of packing. The following day I said goodbye and drove south for my senior year.

What truth did the cloud of that summer reveal? The fear that kept me from following Grandpa Leo to the hospital kept me from ever telling my parents what Grandpa had told me. Why, anyway, would I have said anything? There was no comfort to be had. What Grandpa had endured could not be denied out of existence. And no one, of course, can give any assurance beyond this life. By late October there was snow in the cups of the brittle fallen leaves. I called home Sunday night – it was an odd-numbered Sunday, and my turn – and Dad said a thin film of ice had formed in the bays. We wished each other a good week. The next afternoon, back from the library, I walked in on the phone's sharp ring, a crack of thunder no less terrifying for my having seen the lightning.

Passing

HONK IF YOU LOVE JESUS, the rear bumper commanded, and Jeremy Hanlinson, captaining the Toyota approaching from the Snelling Avenue entrance ramp, complied. He later attributed the ferocity of his horn – three blasts, short-short-long – to the encouragement he was receiving from his riders, encouragement that exploded into raucous laughter when Jeremy pulled even with the forest green minivan in time to see a scowling female face and a defiant middle finger. The van's horn answered, followed by a few swerving lane changes and then, from behind the dueling teenagers, the sudden punch line of flashing red lights.

Jeremy's passengers, Nick Paddock and Brandon Johnston, wrote a song about their adventures and, calling themselves Partners in Crime, performed "The Ballad of the Forest Green Van" at the senior class talent show. They dedicated the song, all three chords, to Our Brave Hero Whose Identity Is Not To Be Revealed; Jeremy, buried deep in the audience, was grateful for the anonymity. "Has anyone asked if it was you who drove that afternoon?" Brandon asked a few days later.

"No. Why would anyone ask?"

"Why *wouldn't* they? They see the three of us together in school."

"Jeremy's not the type," Nick chimed in, which was true. Jeremy's view of the world – of people – was not the view of his two friends.

"All I did was drive, anyway. And pay the fine. I was lucky my license wasn't taken away. Honking wasn't my idea. The Jesus stuff, the pick-up line – that was you two, not me."

"Indeed," Brandon roared. "*Face*. Oh, I liked that giant."

Jeremy had known, while watching the patrolman rise from his open door, that he was about to suffer the consequences of his friends' exuberance. They had persuaded him to honk. And it had been Nick, while the four teenagers had stood outside the patrolman's car, who had evaluated the impressively tall driver of the van and said, casually: "You like to have opinions, don't you?"

She had glowered at him and then glanced toward the patrolman, who had returned to his car to check license plate numbers. "What?"

"We only followed orders." Nick wagged his head toward the bumper sticker.

"That's my mother's, you creep."

Nick had glanced at Brandon, then Jeremy, and smiled without caution. "Jesus mingled with the unwashed."

"Creep."

Then it had been Brandon's turn. "Do you like music? Nick and I here play guitar." A pause. "Or isn't it your thing?"

The girl – she had to be six-two, Jeremy estimated, her surprisingly small face and long, straight, blond hair bringing to mind a comet – had watched Brandon carefully before replying, with deliberation: "Great big dogs fight animals. *Face*."

"Did you say it only to aggravate her?" Jeremy asked Brandon later. "We were in enough trouble as it was."

"Aggravate her?" Brandon tried to look wounded.

"We were only making conversation," Nick said.

Jeremy had seen it often. When the three of them were at the mall it was Brandon or Nick who sought out classmates; to Jeremy, who found keeping up with two friends challenging enough, greeting others was a distraction. At the movies it was the same: how many Friday nights had they entered the ten-screen complex as three and wound up in a group of a dozen, many of whom Jeremy couldn't even name? To Brandon and

Nick the gap between stranger and acquaintance was small, and between acquaintance and friend even smaller.

Jeremy thought of himself as neither unfriendly nor shy. Interaction simply required energy without reward. Once he and Nick had been waiting for an elevator at a mall parking garage when both doors opened simultaneously. Jeremy started for the empty car before following Nick into the car occupied by two boys and two girls only vaguely familiar from school. "Howdy, all," Nick had called in greeting.

After high school Jeremy left the Twin Cities for Madison while Nick and Brandon became roommates at a small liberal arts school south of Minneapolis. Jeremy was looking for a business degree. The constant through his first months at college was loneliness, but gradually the loneliness – Jeremy came to Madison knowing no one – evolved into a sort of soulless freedom. The university was large and vibrant enough to allow Jeremy to run his life without scrutiny. During spring break he visited Nick and Brandon and was astounded by the petri dish quality of their campus. Everyone saw everyone doing everything: eating meals, passing between classes, doing laundry, tapping home on a laptop from the benches along the small muddy river that slid past the humanities building.

He moved into an enormous student house during his sophomore year: nine partitioned bedrooms for nine students. By this time Jeremy had successfully created a world he was comfortable in, a world distant from the whole of-a-piece existence – senior high hierarchy lacquered over with television culture and the chatter of disc jockey shtick – he had lived in suburban St. Paul. Jeremy stepped sideways into the economics program, making friends with the small group he helped edit the department newsletter. He made his meals on *his* schedule, fit in his one-ninth of the household chores. He began to run each morning, putting in five miles along the lakes and through the student neighborhoods. Jeremy enjoyed the continuous churning: Madison, being a college town, was populated with both new arrivals and those preparing to leave.

Brandon telephoned around nine one early December Friday night. "What's your Christmas schedule?" he asked. This was in the boys' junior year. "I'll be back in the Cities by the eighteenth, but Nick's got exams right up to the twenty-third."

"I've got the worst of all finals schedules. Three on the first two days and then one on the last. I won't be home any sooner than Nick."

"Really?" The disappointment was evident. "Listen, I've got an inspiration. I'll come over and get you. We can pack your stuff in my truck and you can save the miles on your car. It'll be a road trip."

"Don't bother. My car can use the miles." A solitary four-and-a-half-hour drive back to Minnesota seemed to Jeremy a reward for surviving finals week. "And I need the car to drive back on the twenty-seventh, anyway."

"Why so short a break?"

"I've got my own road trip, Brandon. After Christmas I'll be accompanying the lovely Aimee Dahl to her hometown of Chicago, Illinois."

This was a revelation. "And she is – " Brandon said casually.

"A journalism major."

"Her parents live in Chicago?"

"They do." In the background a vague and undisciplined chorus of voices was abruptly replaced by a pulsing beat and united but muffled approval.

"And you say you are going with her to this very same Chicago?"

"I do and I am."

"Some revisions are necessary, brother." This brought something to mind, and Brandon proceeded to tell Jeremy about the pharmaceutical commercial he had recently seen: a shyness pill was now on the market, designed to make the patient feel bolder, more confident, at ease among strangers. But the mandated disclosure of side effects had included, among so many other things, possible sexual dysfunction. "Nick and I had fun with that for a week," Brandon said. "I mean, what's the point?"

Jeremy laughed in spite of himself: shyness had never been the issue, not really. "So what does that commercial have to do with me?" he challenged Brandon.

"Nothing, apparently." Brandon slipped easily into the next subject. "Nick made use again of the giant in the forest green van."

"Oh?" The reference took a moment to register.

"Monday night is open mic at this bar comedy club sort of place in town, and he jumped up on stage and worked that story over pretty well."

"You can't miss with good material."

"That's what I said." Brandon detected a ripple of laughter that had risen into Jeremy's bedroom. "Is there a party at your house?"

"Yes'm. I'd say there are sixty people downstairs." Jeremy said this without disapproval. He enjoyed the protection of nearby activity. The loud CD player and the beer and laughter, coupled with the hidden listening post of his bedroom, comforted Jeremy. The waterfall of activity from his housemates' Friday night parties offered a defense against solitude's tendency toward brooding. It carried no obligations.

"Then I'll let you go."

"Don't bother. I enjoy these parties more from up here. I might stop down later."

"That's crazy. There's always time to be alone."

"It's all pretty pointless, Brandon. These people will be dead in a hundred years."

"Precisely. Get down there. But first tell me more about . . . Annie?"

"Aimee." She had been introduced in early November by a friend of Jeremy's from the economics department. Though a year older than Jeremy, she was scheduled to graduate the same spring. Aimee carried the minimum number of credits and spent much of her time at the offices of the student newspaper. "I'm in charge of editorial page coordination and letters to the editor," she had said upon meeting Jeremy. "Last month we received a doozy."

Doozy, charming but clearly an affectation, had made Jeremy take a closer look. Aimee had thick black hair – hair upon a head of hair, to all appearances – and an unnaturally clear and colorless face. A tiny nose supported delicate wire glasses perched well below eyes that had a look of restlessness. Jeremy grasped intuitively that her desirability was the rough equivalent of his.

"You never saw that letter in print," Aimee continued, "for one simple reason. It was a suicide note." She paused for effect. Jeremy felt a slight annoyance, even made the most tentative of moral judgments, at the quiet theatrics.

"You were convinced it wasn't a prank?"

"With certainty." She leaned toward Jeremy and lowered her voice, as though parting with a secret. "He was dead before we received the letter. He was dead and we knew he was dead. His roommate found him the afternoon before and the story was on the radio the day his letter was delivered."

Aimee, full of words, entertained Jeremy. She knew a good paragraph about everyone they met; Jeremy didn't even try to keep it all in memory. She knew everything that was happening: which prof was mulling retirement, how the school's rezoning permit for the new dorms was progressing, the effect of the city's new budget on bus fares. Aimee was offering to make a foreign language easy for Jeremy, it seemed, and Jeremy eagerly accepted – for he was full of words, too, now, all of them for her.

But on the night before Jeremy's drive back to Minnesota, Aimee said, softly and deliberately, "Tell me what you see happening to us." Jeremy heard the notes but not the pitch. He saw them fending off the world. Leaving Madison as soon as they had their degrees and going . . . somewhere. Not to Chicago and not to Minnesota, but some place where they could devote themselves to each other, oblivious to economics and journalism and the distraction of casual acquaintances, chatter, the aimlessness of human activity.

"I like human activity."

"The weekend before Thanksgiving," Jeremy said passionately. "That's what I'm talking about." They had holed themselves up in Aimee's efficiency from three Friday afternoon until noon Sunday. "What else do we need?"

There was something to be said for such a view, Aimee allowed. But she loved Madison and would mourn graduation. *He* had been the distraction, one might say – a nice distraction, of course, she smiled. She pointed out how much life even their little Madison held, and how quickly a lifetime uses itself up; and then, embarrassed, she stopped talking.

The following day Jeremy wrote the last of his exams – "Statistical Applications to Economic Models"; forty-three students scribbled away for ninety minutes, the afternoon's most frenzied activity on a campus that was, only two days before Christmas, largely deserted – and then drove west through the early twilight. He rewrote the exam for a while but by darkness, with St. Paul still three hours distant, tried again to determine what the previous night had meant. The trip to Chicago was in doubt, certainly: Aimee had said she'd call Christmas Day about that. Distraction had been the theme of the evening, and Jeremy kept coming back to it. *I like human activity.* Then again, what was to be made of her exit? Aimee had turned around, half out the doorway, and with a tender smile had teased him with a sing-song melody, apparently concocted on the spot: *People go through this world in twos, and no one tells them they're supposed to . . . .*

No one tells people *anything*, of course – econ had taught Jeremy that. Billions on the planet, all fending for themselves. From the interstate he could see a church here, a farmhouse there, billboards, the recurring pulse of light from a rural airport. And yet people clump together – Jeremy had spent much of the semester studying monolithic buying habits and economic migrations. He thought of a girl from freshman year who had received news from home over her phone one afternoon. The dorm janitor, who hadn't said a word to this girl all year – had probably never given her a thought – heard sobs, turned to see the girl, and embraced her immediately. And she had clamped her arms around him and cried a long and searing moan. The memory was interrupted by an unexpected spray of snow, and then Jeremy's thoughts returned to Aimee. He remembered the way she had looked the first time he saw her, just seven weeks earlier, before he knew anything about her newspaper job or friends or family, the whole complex mix and history carried behind those miniature wire glasses.

When Jeremy moved back to the Twin Cities a year and a half later, college degree securely in hand, his plans were unsettled. The job market was deteriorating. A late application to a masters program was pending. Brandon was still at school, preparing for an extra semester. Nick had graduated, though, and lined up some sort of project that put him on the University of Minnesota campus for the summer. He leased a worn condominium a mile from the East Bank and invited Jeremy in to help with the rent. This was Jeremy's best and only option: his parents had a year earlier taken a premature retirement to Lake Havasu City. Aimee was still in Madison, or at least her name remained on the paper's editorial page roster. Jeremy hadn't seen her since a chance meeting the previous winter.

A week or two after his return, on a morning run that took him across the Washington Avenue Bridge and toward the West Bank hospitals, Jeremy spotted the forest green minivan. The bumper sticker was still on display – indeed, it was the thing that caught Jeremy's attention and made him certain this was the van he had followed four years earlier. Rust had eaten severely into the van and a startling amount of paint had flaked away. Jeremy turned up the sidewalk that climbed the hill overlooking the river. In a slight depression that was the third corner of a triangle joining the parking lot and one of the hospital entrances, a bench appeared in the shade beneath an enormous oak bright with the soft green of June. The van's driver was crouched over on the bench.

Her size alone dispelled all doubt that this was the girl Jeremy had encountered off the Snelling ramp. He lowered his head as he passed the bench, but caught sight for an instant of the disproportionately small face and the lifeless blond hair, now cut short. Her eyes were cast down; she saw nothing. Jeremy's gait took him over the next rise a few seconds later and he ran down the long incline toward Riverside Park.

He knew immediately – or twenty seconds after immediately, as it wasn't until the ambulance garages east of the hospital that he began to tremble with excitement – that he should have stopped. Certainly the anger flashing outside the patrol car would have long ago evaporated. *Face*: that had been genuinely funny, and then there had followed the talent show and years of jokes, bumper sticker and van references. Communicating this seemed, in a way Jeremy couldn't readily understand, a correction. If Jeremy believed in fate, it was the fate of impersonal and predictable market forces, the fate of self-interest. But simply passing anonymously by would surely be an unalterable mistake.

Jeremy circled through the park, allowing his thoughts to settle. He looped back along an empty soccer field and climbed the hill past a row of gray, sharply-pitched townhomes. He thought, suddenly, of his father – or, rather, of his father as he had observed him years earlier, a man who navigated easily a world Jeremy, entering his teenage years, was beginning to find anarchic.

Jeremy emerged on the sidewalk along the avenue, river in view, and closed in on the hospital parking lot. He saw from a distance that the van was gone, its vacant spot conspicuous on a weekday morning. With alarm Jeremy accelerated as he turned up the sidewalk ascending the hill. He sailed over the last rise; the bench was upon him more quickly than he had expected. Jeremy came to a stop over it, looked hard at the brightly-painted blue slats as he caught his breath, examined the empty bench. Almost empty: a thin wisp of tissue, promiscuous as an open letter, turned gently in the soft wake of Jeremy's approach, weighted only by the hard wrinkle of drying tears.

Roeschler's Home

Mark Fletcher's hometown had had a lawyer, but not the kind of lawyer Fletcher was now. In New Hamburg, twenty or more years ago, the community lawyer had already been in practice for decades, drafting deeds and wills and filing pleadings from a storefront office wedged between the drugstore and what had been, through Fletcher's childhood, variously a flower shop, a chiropractor's office, and a pizzeria. When Fletcher was in law school Amos Berbig had suggested selling him his lease and law books, but nothing came of it and Berbig eventually slipped into retirement, his modest prosperity sufficient to deliver him to Fort Smith, Arkansas, two-thirds of the way to warmth. New Hamburg was left without a lawyer. Fletcher finished near the top of his class and settled into an office so high above the Minneapolis street that high school friends asked if he was able, on clear days, to see New Hamburg from forty-five miles.

As the years passed, Fletcher's practice narrowed itself to machinations involving Section 1031 of the Internal Revenue Code. The joke in Fletcher's office – in *part* of his office, since a New Hamburg-sized town of lawyers populated the firm – was that Congress would one day repeal Section 1031 and send Fletcher back to a Berbig of a practice in his hometown. Casual acquaintances often assumed this was the practice Fletcher already had: not infrequently did he receive calls from a suburban neighbor or a college classmate or a parent of one of his wife's students, followed by a request to probate an estate or settle a backyard boundary dispute. Occasionally the stories were exotic – the roommate from sophomore year who had found lyrics, handwritten and familiar, behind the attic wall, or the junior pastor who had bit on an Internet scam and lost his credit card numbers while trying to help spring money out of Zimbabwe. None of these entanglements had anything to do with Section 1031 of the Internal Revenue Code, and Fletcher either referred them to other regions of the firm or told his callers they didn't have the sort of problem a lawyer could do much about.

When Periwinkle Melander phoned, it was the first time Fletcher had heard from or even thought of him since shortly after their graduation with thirty-seven classmates from New Hamburg's high school. Fletcher had left town and Periwinkle had stayed, inheriting his father's three-hundred-twenty-acre dairy farm. "Do you remember our farm?" he asked. "I'm talking about the thing that makes it unique."

Fletcher didn't remember, not at first. "Is it the pond?" he said. "Didn't we once pan for gold there?" Periwinkle laughed sharply at the memory and then Fletcher abruptly recalled the thing Periwinkle almost certainly had in mind. A hundred yards back from the county road stood a rectangle of thick brush, an island among the gently-rolling field corn. There may even have been an arthritic oak watching guard. The tangle of vegetation was the size of a gravesite – *was*, literally, a gravesite. Most every New Hamburg child of Fletcher's generation knew the story: the farm's pioneer homesteader, dead a hundred years, was buried on the spot and the deed to the farm protected the gravesite from disturbance.

"You're talking about the pioneer grave," Fletcher said. "It's still there, I take it. I suppose it *has* to still be there."

"'In perpetuity' is how the easement deed puts it. I'm holding it in front of me now. 'Reserving for Anna Roeschler and her heirs, in perpetuity, an easement over the following-described tract for the maintenance of the gravesite of Adolph Roeschler, buried April 7, 1879.' The easement itself is from the same year. July 24, 1879."

"Really." An assembly line of legal documents crossed

Fletcher's desk each week, but he was unaccustomed to thinking of them as historical curiosities. "With Adolph dead and buried, his widow couldn't work the farm and left. I suppose that's how it happened."

"Farming was tough then and it's no better now," Periwinkle said. "My dad bought this place when I was too young to remember and by the time I joined him in partnership it *still* hadn't been paid off. He's been dead for years now and I've got three daughters and can't see even one more generation for this farm."

"You're looking to sell."

"New Hamburg's changed a lot since we were in school. Do you get back much, Mark? There's a wave of new houses being built and it's on the verge of hitting here. Big, monstrous houses, four and five thousand square feet. So I need a way to break that easement."

The conversation's sudden turn – pioneer homestead rolling into exurban jumbo homes, a measured doggedness in Periwinkle's voice – momentarily dazed Fletcher. "You think a developer would object to the gravesite?"

"A developer *has* objected. He's willing to pay a boatload of money for pasture, Mark. Make me a partner. But not if he can't build on it."

"We'll need to think about this." Fletcher considered the familiar smear of sunlight reflected off great panels of glass across and high above the avenue. "Why don't you come downtown."

"I can come whenever you can fit in an appointment. But you see where I'm coming from, don't you Mark? I can't have my fate determined by someone who has been dead a century." Periwinkle's voice quickened. In self-recognition he forced a mirthless laugh. "I mean, we can't have bones impeding progress, can we?"

Periwinkle arrived the following week with the easement – handwritten and surprisingly well-preserved – and the developer's plans, which Fletcher unrolled across a large table in one of the firm's auxiliary conference rooms. "'Pioneer Homesites,'" Fletcher read, acknowledging with an ambiguous smile the weatherworn audacity of naming a development after the thing intended to be replaced.

"It's a working title. We'll probably end up with something like 'Autumn Valley' or 'Vista Hills.'" There was no irony in Periwinkle's voice, only the dead earnestness of a new endeavor.

"Where is the gravesite?"

Periwinkle pointed to a circle designated *Melissa Lane*. "Under Melissa's cul de sac."

"Does it necessarily have to be disturbed? Your developer could build around it, the way you farm around it now."

Periwinkle gave Fletcher an uncertain smile. He looked much as he had in high school, his entire face built around the distinctive eyes whose color had long ago given him his nickname. "Leave it there? Like a broken-down tractor?"

"It's unique. It would have appeal. Like a monument."

Periwinkle shook his head. "Henderson about got up to leave the first time he learned of the grave. He said it meant nothing but delay. Environmental impact statements and groundwater monitoring wells and maybe some sort of historical designation."

"That may be true in any case. Removing a grave is likely more difficult than preserving it."

The doubt in Fletcher's voice hardened his old classmate's resolve. "First things first," Periwinkle said. "I need you to tell me we can disregard this easement." He handed the curled sheet to Fletcher with a palpable disdain for the slight document's power over him.

"Someone here can give you an answer to that question. It isn't really my area," Fletcher said, as though gravesite easements might actually be an area of specialization. "I'll have someone work on it and then I'll call you in a few days."

"It's not so much knowing the answer," Periwinkle said, musing aloud for Fletcher's benefit. "But you're right, doing the research would be . . ." He paused, then rallied to find the word he was searching for. "Expected."

* * *

Fletcher's firm hired a dozen new graduates each year. Seven remained from the class arriving two years earlier, and of that group Fletcher thought Sarah Walkman-Holt the most impatient with obstructions to commerce. He explained the facts to her dispassionately, putting a slight emphasis on the language that had been chosen for the easement in those early years of statehood. Only after he had answered all of Sarah's questions did Fletcher permit himself an opinion. "In some ways," he said, "it's a scene right out of Monty Python." Sarah smiled tentatively and nodded.

Her research took small parts of four days. The memorandum, three pages long, was not encouraging. Sarah had found little law and no authority for disregarding the easement and removing Adolph Roeschler. *I'm sorry not to have better news*, she wrote in longhand at the bottom of her memo's last page. And then, triumphantly: *Monty Python – British acting troupe popular a quarter of a century ago. Right?*

Fletcher's call to Periwinkle was brief and businesslike. "Oh, there's no reason to doubt her conclusion," Fletcher said. "Sarah is very thorough."

"So the easement means what it says. 'In perpetuity.'"

"Apparently so. I can't say Sarah's research surprises

me. We're talking about moving a corpse. A judge will have an opinion about that."

Periwinkle was philosophical. "Deep down," he said, calmly and with even a hint of cheer, "I really didn't expect to hear anything different."

* * *

On a Saturday eighteen months later, Fletcher, after logging in a full morning of work, took the elevator down to the parking garage and began an hour-long drive to the rural golf course where his son was about to run in the sectional cross-country meet. The course was in the direction of New Hamburg, and beyond it. Fletcher was buoyed by the deep October sky and, finding himself ahead of schedule, chose the two-lane that curved through the valley leading into New Hamburg. The town had been changeless through Fletcher's youth. Now it introduced itself with a pair of bright drive-through restaurants built since Fletcher's last visit two or three years earlier. Beyond these additions, on a hill perennially stitched into rows of Melander corn, stood the frame of an enormous house.

Fletcher wheeled onto the county road to get a closer look. The Melander farmhouse was unchanged, but its yard was now an island among a churned sea of brown: earthmovers had cut hills and filled swales, tentative roads had laced away the geometry of one hundred thirty years of plowing. A large plywood sign, professionally painted, demanded attention. *Future Site of Roeschler Homesites*, it said clumsily, in green lettering. Then, in red: *Luxurious Country Living. Homes Beginning at $499,000.*

Periwinkle appeared from behind the farmhouse. He was riding a mulching lawnmower, wearing the overalls he had undoubtedly worn when his farm had been a farm. Fletcher parked and stepped out to greet him. "Periwinkle!" he called as he crossed the road. Fletcher made a broad wave toward the chaos beyond the farmyard and, when Periwinkle caught notice, gave an exaggerated, quizzical look.

Periwinkle shut down the lawnmower and stepped off to shake hands. "Looking to build a home?" he said genially, but with a perfunctory smile, as though the novelty of the transformation behind him had burned away quickly.

"So you really did it," Fletcher said in wonder. "Took the big step."

"I saw the light. Planting homes makes a hell of a lot more sense than planting corn."

Fletcher mentioned his son's meet and he and Periwinkle spent a moment calculating the remaining driving time. Then Periwinkle led the way to the compacted access road and the two men walked briskly into Roeschler's Homesites. Fletcher worked hard to recall, from a distance of over two decades, the now-departed farmland: where a fenceline had been, the boundaries of a grove of pasture oak. Periwinkle's narrative was of no help – Periwinkle saw the land as though it were only now, for the first time, being shaped by human plans. "That will be the first phases of homes," he said, pointing to the skeleton form Fletcher had seen from the highway. "The groundwater piping and the wastewater treatment system are almost in, the real work these next few weeks will be completion of curb and gutter." Periwinkle took Fletcher to the top of a gentle rise and pointed out the graceful simplicity, evident even at this stage of construction, of Megan Circle, Michelle Way, and Melissa Lane.

"May I ask or shall I wait to be told?" said Fletcher. "Whatever happened with the gravesite?"

Periwinkle gazed across his land thoughtfully, as though evaluating the progress of a crop at midsummer. "It was the damnedest thing. All that fretting and it came to nothing."

Fletcher waited. "I don't understand."

"The more I thought about it, the less likely it seemed that a body from pioneer days might actually be buried in a cornfield. I mean, we just took it on faith all of these years. As did the people before us.

"So I got my brother-in-law out one day with his backhoe and we took a look." Periwinkle paused to allow Fletcher a moment to digest this information. "And it was as I suspected. An empty grave."

Fletcher looked at Periwinkle doubtfully.

"The whole thing was a story, Mark. I guess." *Guess*, stretched into two syllables, was intended to highlight good faith in the grapple of a hopeless dilemma.

"What do you mean, an empty grave?"

Periwinkle turned back toward the farmhouse and, Fletcher following, the two classmates took a step toward Fletcher's car. "Oh, there may have been something there at one time. But think of what a hundred-odd years of winter and rain will do to a pine-plank casket. If there ever was anything there – I'm not convinced there was – it decayed away a long time before we investigated. Because we didn't find a single thing."

"Really," Fletcher said. He wasn't sure whether he was offended by what Periwinkle had done – no, he decided quickly, he *was* offended – but knew he was irritated at the cloying insincerity. "Melander," he said, turning toward the place he remembered the plot of unruly underbrush to have existed. But he said no more, being unexpectedly distracted by a nostalgia weighted toward loss. New Hamburg – a certain New Hamburg, anyway – had irreversibly slipped away. It had done so under his watch, the same way it had slipped away from Amos Berbig while he worked away on his wills and hand-drawn mortgages, unaware that New Hamburg's children were preparing to leave.

"Let me hear it," said Fletcher suddenly. "What you and your brother-in-law found."

"You're asking as my lawyer? My legal counsel?" Periwinkle studied the sloping that overlay what had once been the contours of the Melanders' pond. He quickly suppressed a darting smile. "Nothing," he said, glancing back toward Fletcher. "Gold."

Market Fair

In those days many of the children who moved into Minneapolis had rarely seen a city. The roommate assigned to Ann wore a stethoscope given as a graduation present. Ann watched Stephanie, wise and beautiful and vivacious despite the oppressive heat, introduce herself to the girls as they arrived. It was the warmest Labor Day in thirty years. The dormitory smelled of paint and disinfectant. Its elevators boomed and exhaust from the traffic below curled into the mattresses. Ann knew Stephanie would be a friend but also a reminder of what she had until then expected of herself.

Ann had wide hips and in warm weather wore yellow and robin's egg blue sundresses. As autumn deepened she adopted jeans and a corduroy jacket that made her look older than a college girl. Her face was soft and round, a sunflower embedded within a nest of luxuriant blond hair. Among the apples at Market Fair a small girl from Africa, unheeded, once reached up to touch Ann's hair.

Ann listened rather than spoke. What she heard was often mystifying: a society around her had somehow, outside her notice, ordered itself. Most every conversation she overheard was built upon a foundation of assumptions that for Ann had remained unresolved. She had difficulty distinguishing the common from the strange, accepting without question an abandoned skateboard as it rolled down the sidewalk along Riverside Avenue, but laughing unexpectedly, even harshly, at a professor in an odd hat. Human interaction seemed devoted to the maneuvering of facades. Betrayed, she waited for the facades to be cast aside.

* * *

The following spring she fell in with a seminary student. A friend of Stephanie's had gone to school with Jeff. His good looks spanned generations: he was what both Ann as a twelve-year-old and her parents, now nearing forty-five, imagined a husband to look like. He was without humor, laughing only as social lubrication. He had had small failures in his twenty-three years but had succeeded in the important things.

Ann sensed that there was something solid in her bearing, comforting in her reluctance. She otherwise could not imagine why Jeff was drawn. Could his interest be in the idea of me, she wondered, rather than me myself?

Ann, he scolded her, though gently. Look at yourself.

She did, truly curious. She stood before a floor-length mirror in the dormitory bathroom one night and looked at herself as Jeff might have, seeing her for the first time. There was no denying it. There was no denying the beauty.

* * *

She was awarded, the following year, one of ten places in a poetry seminar. The professor riffed on sentimentalism. It can be measured in the culture, he said, by the names we give our children. He said this with a flourish, fueled by his own momentum. I often chuckle to think of Ann, for example, consciously simple, agrarian, pretentious in its unpretension. He stopped, stricken. A thought had occurred. He lowered his eyes to Ann. Don't tell me, he said. It was only the second week and the names were beginning to settle in. You're Ann, aren't you.

She smiled but preserved his discomfort a few more moments before answering. Ted specified this when he introduced himself at class end. That was masterful, he said.

They had seen one another around campus. They had mutual friends. Why are you called Ted, she asked, when your name isn't Ted? He told the story of the baseball card given him by an uncle and how he had treasured it so that everyone began to call him Ted, after the card. So you knew I'm not really Ted, he remarked. And I know a little about you.

At Jeff's name a fear seized Ann. She pulled in her hands. She looked toward a low corner of the empty room while he spoke. No, she said, not since the start of summer. Okay, he said cautiously, but she didn't hear anymore, the sounds separating from their meanings and curling off into emptiness.

* * *

She spoke, into the winter and then the following spring, after the seminar had tired and lurched to its conclusion – she spoke of the plays and her job and growing up and what she was learning of Minneapolis. She was spending evenings, Ted gathered, at The Bald Soprano. Had he seen *Sisyphus in Kansas*? He hadn't. In two months *Sisyphus* closed and was followed by *Molotov 7, Unadorned*. Ann answered Ted's questions soberly, without evident enthusiasm. Yes, she said, I enjoy them. Nick is creative. What he does with that theater and that budget is . . . . Her voice trailed off; she was too wary to speak in superlatives. Oh boy, she spurted suddenly in laughter, does he ever think a lot of himself though.

She worked when she could at the day care beside the co-op. They slump their daughters in at 6:30 every morning, she said, white uniforms with grey underarms. Grey underarms, she repeated. Jeff would have disliked me saying that. It was the only time Ted heard her mention Jeff. This morning a glassy eyed mother rolled her bruised son in, she said, ignoring the boy's squareness. They dream on the cots, those children. Dream of the things that once conceived them. Dream, she said abruptly, whether they know it or not, of the regret.

* * *

My grandfather owned a junkyard, Ann said, so I was popular. They were in the cafeteria. A month later Ted remembered the junkyard and asked about it. They were then walking through the small city park that bumped up against the college. Oh yes I was popular, she laughed. He would yell at us from under a car. Hi boys. We were girls. We dared each other to climb into cars we knew people had died in, looking for forgotten bodies. Sometimes we would find a scarf or a dirty mitten and run screaming. At night we woke ourselves with dreams of dirty mittens.

* * *

There are advantages to Nick, she told him. I love the glamour of it. And I love the distance. He's down there all day and night and cares nothing about – she looked out the cafeteria window at the red brick and paper fluttering from a kiosk – about *here*. College, she laughed, shaking her head in bemusement. College.

     She had seemed to Ted unhappy through the fall of the year, each day shorter than the last, the northern plains succumbing to the dark and cold comprehensively. But now the last small ridges of snow glistened in crystals and water ran in the streets and at night rain blew through the trees. She was less frequently solemn, willing even to tease and back away from all the hardships, the classes and rules and expectations and the indifferent future that, though indifferent, regarded Ann with skepticism from all sides. She was able to back away from that. One night Ted watched her use a tablespoon to catapult a fist of whipped cream into Stephanie's hair.

Did I tell you about last Friday? she asked. Nick had a room at Klondike's to celebrate the new show. He introduced me to Louis Powell. She and Ted had listened to Louis in the coffeehouses – he had resurrected the Cats and the Fiddle with their Killer Diller Hep Cat Jive and the Four Vagabonds with their Duke of Dubuque. As flaky in person as he is behind a microphone, she said. Flakier. And that cartoonist was there, too, the one who lost all his funnies when the warehouse burned. There are advantages to it, Ted. Although . . . . Even in the spring there was still an Although.

* * *

She spoke of teaching overseas. South America intrigued her. Africa was a possibility. So much wanderlust for a farmtown girl, he smiled. I suppose, she said, I have Luis to thank for that.

He had never heard mention of Luis. The name had never come up.

Before Nick, she said matter-of-factly. He had been recently arrived from Central America and they had met in a summer class across town. Those first weeks had been intense. We didn't understand each other very well, she giggled. At midsummer he had returned home for six weeks. Every bit of me knew we couldn't survive those six weeks, she said. I looked at my calendar all six weeks, the day circled in red, and went out to the airport and within a minute of seeing his face I knew I had been right. She shook her head sadly, in wonder. What a fool I was for hoping for anything different. But I'm a fool no longer.

* * *

Spring break arrived and the campus packed to leave. Ann allowed herself to regard the journey home as exotic. An ancient history class had put archaeology in her head. Beyond my grandfather's junkyard is a farmhouse, she said, a farmhouse that has been empty since long before anyone conceived of me. Surrounded now by trees. One grows out from a window. There is a root cellar. Ann believed in artifacts buried beneath the foundation.

Will you dig alone? he asked. The smile lingered.

Possibly. She brushed the hair from her eyes. I have a cousin.

Shovels?

Those too.

Ice picks?

She looked up. It was Thursday night. The pleasures of the coming week, triumphant entry to resurrection, would never be as strong as now, and in two syllables he had blasted those pleasures jagged.

It won't work, will it? The blood seemed to drain from her face. At home the frost's still in the ground.

Maybe not.

Of course it is. She had been loading her suitcase but now sat down. I've been acting like an idiot. I feel stupid.

No. The idea's still good.

But the idea, good or not, had passed. I've been acting, she said, like a little child. She stared far away, as she had that first afternoon at class end.

The transformation frightened him. It's nothing, Ann. Nothing has changed.

What, she said. What in the world could I have been thinking.

* * *

Summer found her living in a brick house, dark and ancient, two miles north of campus. Her room was at the top of a long and steep flight of stairs that began inside the entryway. Ted came back to town and early one evening found Ann in her rocking chair, a lime green sundress falling to her thick ankles and bare feet, brown but for the white cross of sandal tan lines. Her hair, glorious in the humidity, had lost its corn silk yellow to the bleaching sun. The curtains were drawn to preserve the attic coolness. Water beaded upon a nearby glass of iced tea.

They walked back toward school instinctively. Nostalgia, already, was settling in on his part, restlessness on hers. They talked about books. She advocated for the Brontës and Lessing, he for Fitzgerald and Roth.

She mentioned a dream. I was caught in a robbery. A bullet went through my heart and I knew I was supposed to be dead so I let myself down to the floor and closed my eyes even though I felt normal. She giggled. Normal.

She had a story about her girls. You should have seen us last week, she said. Through the summer she took city girls north to the St. Croix and they canoed their way down through the leaning trees and sandbars. It was so hot, Ted, the way it has been all summer, and we took our shirts off, everything, we were regular Amazons.

With high school girls?

These are tough kids. Not like your girls.

You'll amazon yourself out of a job. Maybe into prison. You'll be on television.

We all said that, Sheila and the other counselors. She laughed defiantly. We did it anyway.

She asked about what she called his love life. He was spending the summer back home. Don't you get married on me, she said. But if you do there better not be another best man. I want that job.

Do you know what I really want? she said later. I want one of my sisters to get married and have a big wedding back home. I want everyone to be there but me. And during the reception my sister will stand before the crowd and read aloud my letter of congratulations and best wishes. And that's how everyone will know. Imagine that. Ann in Africa.

* * *

There were things he did not learn until much later. Her younger sister, still at home, had written for help. It's natural to feel sad, Ann had written back. There's a lot of pressure on a 16-year-old. There are 3 things to do when you feel sad. 1. Talk to someone. 2. Go out and do something nice for someone else (write Ann a letter). 3. Make a list of all the nice things about yourself!! (cheat a little!)

I used to do that. I sat down and wrote things like . . . Ann is smart. Ann has a good family. Ann cares about people. Ann has pretty hair. Ann is going to travel all over the world!!

I'm proud of you! It's hard to give advice in a letter. It sounds too much like preaching, but you know I never preach!

I need your letters to cheer me up! As often as you cry, I think you are basically a very strong person. I have faith in you. I love you. I love you.

* * *

She asked Ted, as the school year's first weekend arrived, to accompany her to The Bald Soprano. The theater, six blocks from campus, was housed in a discarded fire hall. Three small sections of bleachers, each half a dozen rows high, surrounded a stage scarcely larger than a dormitory room. The Bald Soprano, a favorite with the local press, was nearly full. Ted and Ann sat in the back and off to one side. The audience held a few suits, a few students, a number of people whom Ann identified as actors she had seen at Nick's parties.

The play was *Chromosomorama*. Three men, using their male voices but speaking the experience of women, conversed with three women who, though dressed and groomed as women, played the parts of men. All six sat in a subway car that for the duration of the performance rocked to and fro by virtue of ropes pulled by volunteers from the audience. The reception was enthusiastic and after the curtainless curtain call the crowd remained standing and chanted with irony for Nick.

He was short and perhaps thirty years old. He sprang onto the stage like a cat, a cat who wore sandals, white pants flecked with paint, a Hawaiian shirt, and a broad panama. He wore a black beard cropped close that ran high up the cheek.

She brought Ted forward to meet Nick after the crowd had dispersed. Nick still vibrated with the thrill of the evening's performance. He smiled at Ted with long teeth. You're at the college with Ann? he asked. Could I enlist you to help spread the word about us down here?

Ted allowed Ann and Nick their conversation by examining a *Sisyphus in Kansas* poster on the far wall. The theater walls had been painted black. He studied the poster slowly, the multitude of names and dates, then finished and began again, this time more slowly yet.

She approached him eventually. I think I'm going to stay. You don't mind? They looked back toward the stage where Nick had now joined two men in inspecting a strip of lumber that during the performance had rattled loose from the subway car. All three men held hammers and were laughing. Playing, she smiled. Nothing but boys.

* * *

I could have married my high school sweetheart, she said one night. *Some Like It Hot* had been on television and she and Stephanie and Ted had watched it while drinking beers. Now the movie was over and Stephanie was upstairs, settling into organic chemistry.

He asked me. But he asked me because he needed a farm wife. Eighteen years old and already trapped. She shook her head sadly. Tell me again about Lynn.

Just a high school girl.

And your prom was in a gravel pit? She laughed from deep inside.

The party afterwards was.

He had a potato skin face, she said later. I laughed when he asked me. She looked hard at Ted. Who was I to laugh?

* * *

He would sometimes see her daily and other times not for a week or more. His telephone rang one night and the sorrow gathering so long at a distance had arrived.

They march them out in uniforms, she cried. Her tears were unmistakable. And they line them in their rows and they chant to God, all in unison. She choked bitterly. Then they recite. They hear a line from the principal and repeat it. Hear another and repeat it. Oh, Ted, it's hateful. It's *shit*.

The call came during the evening of his first night back at school after mid-fall's three-day break. That's what that sort of school is like, he said. That's what it *is*.

I can't abide by that. Her words burned.

Your students might not either, he said, searching. He consciously calmed himself against her anguish. Kids have their own minds, Ann, even at that age. They'll be alright.

Uniforms. And they line them in rows and they sing and it's all because someone tells them to do it. And they *recite*.

I hear you.

I can't abide by any of it. The sentence began in rage, even at him, and rose to a wild despair.

Stephanie approached him in the cafeteria the following evening, Wednesday. October's sunlight penetrated the room flatly, dust floating through like sea fog. She called in ill to the school but left anyway, Stephanie said. Have you heard from her at all? *At all* betrayed her alarm. Did she tell you anything last night? Stephanie's eyes told Ted she had abandoned her instinctive optimism.

Near ten o'clock he crossed to the small house Stephanie and Ann had found at campus's edge. He imagined Stephanie abashed upon seeing him at the door. *I should have called you, Ted. I was just so relieved when she finally returned.* But she was not abashed. No, she said, nothing. Nothing.

He felt, through the night, a confusion, a restlessness that pitched him between horror, guilt, and denial. He had never known what tragedy might be like. Once on Christmas Eve his grandparents had arrived two hours late. He had convinced himself, had pictured vividly the overturned car and ambulance. He could no longer remember the particulars of it. They had appeared with gifts and warmth, smiling as they stomped the snow off their rubber boots like flakes off a pastry. Another life, a dreaded life, had been avoided and was soon forgotten. All night the phone did not ring and he believed that his other life had begun.

He waited all Thursday, one listless class to another, each hour without news of calamity a bud of permission to hope. He heard no grim news from Stephanie, saw nothing of her at all; but he saw nothing of Ann either. Two thousand students remained after Ann and yet the campus had become a different place. In the entire world, among civilizations of peoples, two thousand had chosen their way here and Ted couldn't remember why he was one of them. He had come to be seared.

Stephanie telephoned as he returned from dinner. When he arrived she was waiting at the door. They entered together. She spoke pleasantries for Ann's benefit but kept meaningful eyes on Ted. She watched him sit on the second couch and then left the room.

Ann sat in her yellow dress. He knew her wardrobe as well as she. Her legs were folded beneath her and she watched him without expression. The television was off, the music also, and there wasn't a book or magazine in the room. Two boys kicked a football back and forth in the street outside the house. Each kick sounded like an axe into a tree and after moments of suspension came the sound of heavy descent, the ball hitting the street or hard lawn crazily, sometimes near, sometimes far.

She spoke perfunctorily long after Stephanie had left the room. Asking about this class or that, a brother of his back home, blinking when he remarked upon the weather over mid-fall. Both were quietly obedient to one another. There were long silences and in one of the silences they heard Stephanie close the house's back door behind her.

I went to Market Fair after our phone call, she said. I bought cold medicine and sleeping pills and a dozen eggs. She laughed softly as an acknowledgment that buying the eggs could in some circumstances be deemed something deserving of laughter. So as to not arouse suspicion, she said. I sat on the bus bench outside the store and wrote my long note. The next morning I went across town to Nick's apartment.

He hardly breathed. His arms and thighs ached with the tightness. He had frequently, through his entire life, gone to sleep as one person and woken as another. But she was telling him that the solitude and reconsideration and new day, Tuesday becoming Wednesday, had not effected any change on her. His palm became red and creased against the heavy oak arm of the couch.

I let myself in and took the pills, forty-four of them. Twenty-four sleeping pills and twenty cold pills. So, he thought, wondering what it meant that she had counted. I then laid myself down on his couch.

He stared at her dumbly. Yesterday morning, he said.

Nine o'clock, she answered. Ten o'clock. Outside the football rattled hard off a bike rack. And did not wake until ten last night. She smiled the slightest smile in wonder.

Did Nick find you?

Nick was rehearsing all day. I got up and called the hospital. The danger had passed over me. Like a cloud, Ted. Like a cloud sliding beneath the sun. I came home after Stephanie was asleep, got in bed, and couldn't rouse myself when morning came. Could hardly do it this afternoon, for that matter.

He doesn't know?

He's the only one who does know. And you. I went down to the theater at four. I told him and then I came home. She looked out the window. Stephanie doesn't know.

You should call someone.

She turned back toward him meekly, waiting for instructions, willing to submit. A crisis center or somewhere, he said.

Before going to see Nick this afternoon I called suicide prevention.

He watched her face closely. Did you?

She seemed to expect the skip in rhythm, the skepticism. She nodded and waited for approval.

That's good. A tumult warred inside him, fear at her single-mindedness and capacity, gratitude for this new compliancy. She herself had been badly frightened and he fought strongly the instinctual temptation to reassure, to reaffirm, to rehabilitate her into the Ann who had felt compelled to visit Market Fair.

I called suicide prevention and I called Mary Roberts about teaching. It wasn't anything at all. She told me to just call her when I was ready to go back.

She looked at him fearfully. I'm not going back.

I don't know why it happened. It's just that . . . . She pushed the thought away. They sat for a long time without speaking as the room sank into the gathering dusk.

I'm determined, she said abruptly. I am, Ted. I'm going to treat this as . . . .

A warning, he said.

She nodded absently.

* * *

For a week he visited her every night. He entered and chatted with Stephanie, sometimes helping her clean up the kitchen. Ann listened. She did not smile but enjoyed hearing them talk.

After Stephanie left for the library Ann and Ted slipped into jackets and took the long walk down the Washington Avenue Bridge. To their left was the graffiti, a geography lesson of national involvement. Fliers batted in the wind that had arisen with the sun's tumble into the trees. Fliers for the pregnant. Fliers for the addicted. Louis Powell at Seven Corners. There were fliers, too, for the sad, the lonely, the discouraged, the despairing. A lot of different words, he observed. Like Eskimos and their words for snow. She stared without opinion.

To their right was the river, gray and sliding far beneath. Berryman's bridge, they knew. After hearing the story they had once leaned over the railing and speculated.

He told her about his day, each oddity. She enjoyed the stories, though the students and professors were no longer anything more than characters, props. She had little to tell, not having returned to her classes and unsure what would become of student teaching. I had my appointment, she offered.

I imagine, he said bravely, you have thought quite a bit about last Wednesday.

She answered immediately. Oh yes. As though failing to convince him would doom both of them. I try to analyze it. It's just . . . . I don't know. She tried again. That school, everything about it, it broke me. She looked at him as though being broken was the last thing she had expected. I saw everything for what it is. There didn't seem to be any hope, Ted. The thing I'd been trying all my life to attain is a thing that only wants to destroy me.

She didn't expect an answer and this gave him time to plan and measure his words. So what. If that school wants to be more a prison than a school, let it. You're free of it, Ann. Don't put your eggs in that basket.

That's what I learned today, she said. Eggs in a basket. My counselor said those exact words.

* * *

She was surprised to see him each night but not displeased. The weekend had warmed into a brief second summer and on Monday, the fifth evening, the sunlight angled off the water's surface. Orange traced the treetops and insects bubbled through air fragrant with decaying leaves and thin blue smoke.

You were quoted today, she said. About keeping perspective. Didn't you say that? My counselor spoke it almost exactly as you had and I told him that. I said I had heard it from a friend. Ann, he told me, you have a wise friend.

Ted enjoyed the tease, though it wasn't a tease. Well, he said. When they reached the far end of the bridge they crossed over and came back on the other side, looking upriver. Presently they stepped down into the neighborhood, the partitioned houses and ivy-draped church wedged in by student lots. They crossed Riverside Avenue and mounted the porch.

I don't know what you've been trying to do, she said, giving him a grateful and quizzical look. But thank you.

I haven't been trying to do anything.

That note I composed outside Market Fair, she started.

On the bench, he said.

I wrote it to you.

He was conscious of regret, of fear, of even a murmur of thrill. He refused to acknowledge their presence.

What other friend, she said, do I have?

He wished her goodnight and waited on the porch until Stephanie's voice could be heard from behind the door. He descended the porch steps and then the small hill to the street and passed the library on his way home. He walked by an open door leading down to a boiler room; a yellow light high up the wall was protected from damage by a cage. The grass in the common was cool and slicked with dew. Lights appeared one by one, then in clusters, across the campus.

The subterranean churning of the boiler room, the chill rising from the lawn, the dormitory window lights declaring themselves like stars – each buried itself in his memory. They lay in waiting through the few remaining Octobers, the three Octobers, then emerged in dark and sinuous commemoration, again and again, his long life thereafter.